# Sharif lifted the baby against his shoulder.

Ben's little head came up, and two shiny eyes peered into his.

Love flooded through Sharif, so powerful that the breath caught in his throat. He could not deny the power that his child held over him. He had thought he could produce a son and then simply entrust him to the women in his family. The child had been intended as a gift to his homeland. Now he knew he would protect the child at any cost.

The bathroom door opened. The fragrance of Holly's hair and the brightness of her spirit filled the room.

She tossed her borrowed shirt onto the bed. "I can wash that by hand...."

"We have a more important matter to—" He stopped, on catching sight of her changed appearance.

"Well?" she asked. "Is it that bad?"

Bad enough that he wanted to resume where they had left off, with a kiss that deepened into something that no man should contemplate with another man's bride....

D0451976

Dear Intrigue Reader,

A brand-new year, the launch of a new millennium, a new cover look—and another exciting lineup of pulse-pounding romance and exhilarating suspense from Harlequin Intrigue!

This month, Amanda Stevens gives new meaning to the phrase "men in uniform" with her new trilogy, GALLAGHER JUSTICE, about a family of Chicago cops. They're tough, tender and totally to die for. Detective John Gallagher draws first blood in *The Littlest Witness* (#549).

If you've never been *Captured by a Sheikh* (#550), you don't know what you're missing! Veteran romance novelist Jacqueline Diamond takes you on a magic carpet ride you'll never forget, when a sheikh comes to claim his son, a baby he's never even seen.

Wouldn't you just love to wake up and have the sexiest man you've ever seen take you and your unborn child into his protection? Well, Harlequin Intrigue author Dani Sinclair does just that when she revisits FOOLS POINT. *My Baby, My Love* (#551) is the second story set in the Maryland town Dani created in her Harlequin Intrigue book *For His Daughter* (#539).

Susan Kearney rounds out the month with a trip to the wildest American frontier—Alaska. *A Night Without End* (#552) is another installment in the Harlequin Intrigue bestselling amnesia promotion A MEMORY AWAY.... This time a woman wakes to find herself in a remote land in the arms of a sexy stranger who claims to be her husband.

And this is just the beginning! We at Harlequin Intrigue are committed to keeping you on the edge of your seat. Thank you for your enthusiastic support.

Sincerely,

Denise O'Sullivan
Associate Senior Editor, Harlequin Intrigue

# Captured by a Sheikh
## Jacqueline Diamond

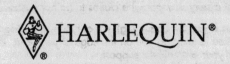

TORONTO • NEW YORK • LONDON
AMSTERDAM • PARIS • SYDNEY • HAMBURG
STOCKHOLM • ATHENS • TOKYO • MILAN • MADRID
PRAGUE • WARSAW • BUDAPEST • AUCKLAND

ISBN 0-373-22550-4

CAPTURED BY A SHEIKH

Copyright © 2000 by Jackie Hyman

Visit us at www.romance.net

**Printed in U.S.A.**

# ABOUT THE AUTHOR

A former news reporter, Jacqueline Diamond has covered the police beat in several cities of Orange County, California, where this book is set. The author of more than twenty-five Harlequin romances, she's married and has two sons.

## Books by Jacqueline Diamond

HARLEQUIN INTRIGUE
435—AND THE BRIDE VANISHES
512—HIS SECRET SON
550—CAPTURED BY A SHEIKH


HARLEQUIN AMERICAN ROMANCE
 79—THE DREAM NEVER DIES
196—AN UNEXPECTED MAN
218—UNLIKELY PARTNERS
239—THE CINDERELLA DARE
270—CAPERS AND RAINBOWS
279—GHOST OF A CHANCE
315—FLIGHT OF MAGIC
351—BY LEAPS AND BOUNDS
406—OLD DREAMS, NEW DREAMS
446—THE TROUBLE WITH TERRY
491—A DANGEROUS GUY
583—THE RUNAWAY BRIDE
615—YOURS, MINE AND OURS
631—THE COWBOY AND THE HEIRESS
642—ONE HUSBAND TOO MANY
645—DEAR LONELY IN LA...
674—MILLION-DOLLAR MOMMY
687—DADDY WARLOCK
716—A REAL-LIVE SHEIKH
734—THE COWBOY AND THE SHOTGUN BRIDE
763—LET'S MAKE A BABY!
791—ASSIGNMENT: GROOM!
804—MISTLETOE DADDY

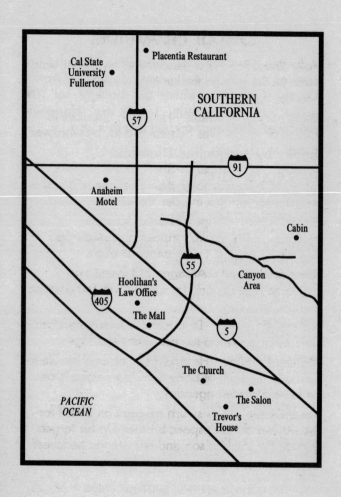

# CAST OF CHARACTERS

*Holly Rivers* — She's a dead ringer for her missing sister. Blood may be thicker than water, and so may deception.

*Sheikh Sharif Al-Khalil* — He doesn't hesitate to take what he believes he's entitled to, by whatever means necessary.

*Jasmine "Jazz" Rivers* — She took the sheikh's money to have his baby, then disappeared. Is she an extortionist, or a murder victim?

*Zahad Adran* — Dispossessed of his own inheritance, the sheikh's trusted aide might be looking to replace it with someone else's.

*Tevor Samuelson* — Attorney, old friend and would-be bridegroom, he invites trust. But does he merit it?

*Noreen Wheaton* — Director of a surrogacy clinic, she's been known to tamper with client files.

*Manuel Estrellas* — He risked his job and his life to tell Holly the truth of baby Ben's parentage. Does he have a hidden agenda?

*Yusuf Gozen* — He's sworn revenge on Sharif for the slaying of his despotic brother. Do his targets include the sheikh's son and the woman he loves?

**Special thanks to Gary Bale and Kelly Millard**

# Prologue

*October*
*Bahrim City, Alqedar, in southern Arabia*

The surrogate mother was gone. And, with her, the baby due to be born in a few weeks.

Furious on hearing the news, Sheikh Sharif Al-Khalil clenched his fists. "The police in California—will they not help?"

Zahad Adran, the sheikh's cousin, aide and chief of security at the palace, spread his hands in frustration. "They have found no signs of foul play, so there is no criminal investigation."

The sheikh stared at his aide over the papers stacked on his broad desk, the contracts that would bring money for hospitals and schools. "I will fly to America at once. I must find my son!"

Beneath his red-and-white-checked kaffiyeh, the traditional headdress of his country, Zahad's scarred face was wise beyond his years. "Cousin, let me deal with this situation. Our people need you, now more than ever."

"The longer we wait, the harder it will be to find

her!'' Sharif could scarcely think beyond the need to retrieve the woman who would bear his child.

"If you approve, I will fly to California tomorrow and investigate," Zahad said. "The director of the surrogacy clinic, Noreen Wheaton, has promised to cooperate. However, we must remember that the mother has many rights under American law."

Angrily, the sheikh turned away. Mirrored in the glass of an arched window, his eyes glittered with rage. His sharp-featured face, hardened by warfare, was softened only slightly by a short beard and mustache, and by the white, banded headcloth that fell across the shoulders of his business suit.

Nine years ago, while Sharif was away fighting to free their country from a dictator, his wife, Yona, had died in childbirth. He would not risk the life of another woman he loved, but he had done his best to produce an heir.

Beyond the window sprawled Bahrim City, the second largest community in the Arabian nation of Alqedar. Its people depended on him. And he, apparently, had depended on the wrong woman. "She has sold herself already. Perhaps she now intends to raise the price."

"If we must bribe the girl, so be it," Zahad said. "Let us hope it is only money she wants, and not custody."

Sharif swung back to face his cousin. Although he had read of custody battles when he was a college student in New York, this personal betrayal outraged him. "She signed a contract and accepted one hundred and fifty thousand dollars!"

"Of which the clinic has received only half pending the child's birth," Zahad reminded him. "In

any case, my friend, we cannot ride in like warriors
and take what is ours. Please allow me to handle this
matter in your stead.''

Reluctantly, Sharif yielded. ''Very well,'' he said.
''You will advise me the moment you learn of her
whereabouts. I'll join you there if this matter cannot
be quickly resolved.''

Zahad bowed, although no such formalities were
necessary between the two men. ''Of course,'' he
said, and retreated.

Sharif reminded himself that his cousin was a capable man. It was, after all, Zahad who had found the
Crestline View Clinic in the first place.

Southern California was one of the world's few lo-
cations that offered high-quality medical facilities, lax
laws regarding surrogate parenting, and a population
of liberated young women. Even so, it had taken Mrs.
Wheaton many tries to find a surrogate who met the
sheikh's high standards.

From the top desk drawer, he withdrew a photograph. It was the woman he knew as H. J. Rivers.

Her face riveted him, the hazel eyes strikingly intelligent within a heart-shaped face. She had dramatic
dark-red hair and a gentle mouth that reminded him
of Yona.

The accompanying description was spare. ''Age
twenty-five, never married, Ms. Rivers works as a
manicurist at a beauty salon and lives with her older
sister. She has sung professionally.

''She wishes to help Your Excellency secure your
people's future, and plans to use the money to make
a demonstration recording to further her singing ca-
reer.''

Mrs. Wheaton's one qualm was that H. J. Rivers

had never previously given birth. Sharif, however, preferred that his son have a virtuous mother. A woman who lived an apparently chaste life, sharing quarters with her sister, suited him well.

Now he wondered whether anything had been omitted or misrepresented. Above all, why had this beautiful woman disappeared with his soon-to-be-born son?

From the desk, he drew the other photograph, the one he had received four months ago. A blurry ultrasound image formed the shape of a baby boy, a son who would enrich his father's life, and those of their people.

Sharif had fallen in love with this child from the moment he saw the picture. How could he bear to lose him?

Suddenly finding it hard to breathe, he threw open the window. Outside the palace, October sunshine baked mud-brick houses, and a breeze carried the aromas of coffee, spices and frankincense from an open-air marketplace. It was a poor city, although rich in tradition.

The entire Arabian nation of Alqedar had its share of economic woes, but it was the fifty-thousand residents of Bahrim City and its environs who concerned Sharif, because they fell under his family's protection. For the first time, prosperity lay within reach.

The region's twisted, pale Jubah trees yielded a silklike fiber prized for its softness and durability. Recently, the fiber had been synthesized under Sharif's patronage.

He owned the patent jointly with chemist Hakem "Harry" Haroun, who was married to Sharif's cousin Amy. Soon large-scale production of Jubah cloth would fund badly needed public works. Then no man, child, or woman of Bahrim would die, as Yona had, for lack of a modern hospital.

All was not secure, however. Other regional leaders eyed the project enviously. Also, Sharif had received death threats for his role in overthrowing the late dictator, Maimun.

The future of Bahrim could not rest on his shoulders alone. He needed an heir. The love he felt for his unborn son had been an unexpected bonus.

The creak of hinges snapped Sharif to attention. Pivoting, he reached for his gun.

"Jumpy as a cat, aren't you?" His aunt Selima glided into the room. In her late sixties, she had a strong, watchful face and black hair distinguished by a shock of silver fanning from a widow's peak. A gold-embroidered crimson dress skimmed her ample figure.

"Has Zahad told you what happened?" he asked, withdrawing his hand from within his jacket.

"Yes, but we must hope for the best." His aunt whisked aside piles of paper to clear a space on his desktop. "You requested my instruction and you shall have it."

"Aunt Selima, this is no time for such matters!"

Ignoring his frown, she unrolled a pad and, from her woven shoulder bag, produced a cherubically naked plastic doll. "Well?" she demanded, holding out a thick, folded cloth. "You won't learn anything standing over there!"

There was no point in fighting the inevitable. With a rueful smile, the sheikh went to take his first lesson in diapering.

# Chapter One

Where had the baby gotten those dark, piercing eyes? Holly Rivers wondered as she gazed down at the child in her arms. Whoever the father was, if he had eyes like those, he must exert a hypnotic appeal.

Little Ben blinked, and the impression of ferocity vanished. When he stretched his tiny arms and yawned, her heart clenched.

She had thought she knew what love was, until the first time this baby was placed in her arms. Then she'd discovered, in a burst of wonder, the true depth of the human heart.

Did he have to be such a chunky fellow at three months, though? Although her arms were beginning to hurt, Holly hesitated to position him any closer against her for fear of spoiling her antique lace wedding dress.

She hoped Alice Frey, her matron of honor and her employer at the Sunshine Lane Salon, would return soon with their flowers. She needed Alice's help to feed Ben before the four-o'clock ceremony, and they only had half an hour left.

"Hey, can I come in?" The question was followed by a belated knock on the partly open door of the church's dressing room. Without waiting for an answer, in marched Trevor Samuelson.

Her groom. The man she was to marry for all the kindness and caring he'd shown over the years, and for the secure home he was offering her and Ben.

Although black and white weren't the most flattering colors for a blond, blue-eyed man, the tuxedo looked handsome on Trevor. "You look terrific," she said, smiling.

"It's not exactly comfortable." With a wry expression, he tugged on the bow tie.

At forty-eight, Trevor, a successful attorney, was eighteen years older than Holly and a longtime friend of her late parents. Until recently, she'd thought of him as a kind of uncle.

Then, during the past year, his friendly manner had shifted into courtship. At first, she'd kept him at arm's length.

But after her pregnant sister Jazz disappeared, Trevor had been her mainstay, offering emotional support and spending his own time and money on the search. It had been a relief to share her burden.

Just before Christmas, one of Jazz's scruffy musician friends, Griffin Goldbar, had showed up with Ben. Astonished at being handed a baby, Holly hadn't questioned him forcefully, especially after Griff assured her that Jazz would return in a few days.

When she didn't, Holly had worried all through Christmas. She'd begun to fear that her sister might not return at all.

Two weeks ago, when Trevor assured her that his love was big enough to include the child, Holly accepted his proposal. Maybe his kisses didn't set her on fire, but she needed him.

She was in no shape, financially or emotionally, to raise a child alone. Besides, he made her feel safe and cherished.

His eagerness had persuaded her not to delay the wedding. Fortunately, she already had her mother's wedding gown.

"Did I mention how stunning you look?" Trevor brushed his thumb across the wing of dark-red hair that fell to her collar. "Honey, I'm just bursting with pride. I can't wait to see you walk down the aisle."

She blushed. "Have many of the guests arrived?" Holly's parents were dead, and she had no other close family. Neither did Trevor, whose childless first marriage had ended in divorce five years ago.

The guests included her co-workers and some of Trevor's colleagues. Many couldn't attend, however, because courts were in session. The wedding had been scheduled on the salon's afternoon off, a Monday, which was also one of the few days the church had been available.

"They're straggling in." The crease deepened in his cheek. "I'm nervous, can you believe that? It's not as if I've never done this before, but it feels like the first time."

"For me, too, Trev," teased Holly, and startled a laugh from her fiancé.

He looped his arm around her and Ben, and angled for a kiss. At that moment, an armful of flowers swept through the door and a penetrating female voice rapped out, "Don't you know it's bad luck for the groom to see the bride before the ceremony? Out! Out!''

''Yes, ma'am.'' With a sigh, Trevor executed a mock bow in Alice's direction, and withdrew.

''How's our darling?'' Alice asked, placing her bouquet on the conference table.

''He said he's nervous.''

''I don't mean Trevor! I mean the baby!'' Alice clucked at Ben, who cooed back at her. ''My goodness, I feel as if you're *my* little grandbaby! I wish my son would get married, but it's beginning to look less and less like he ever will. This may be the only grandchild I ever have, and I don't want to lose him just because you're getting married!''

''Don't worry, Alice. You're as close to Ben as any grandmother could be.'' Holly meant every word.

The short salon owner, who at fifty fought a never-ending battle against gray hair and a thickening waist-line, had adored Ben from the first moment she saw him.

When Holly's finances were strained by the search for her sister, the salon owner had even offered to let the two move into her small house. Thanks to Trevor, however, that wouldn't be necessary.

''You know I like Jazz,'' said Alice, who had put up patiently with the aspiring singer's occasional absences from her manicure duties. ''But if she doesn't care enough about this baby to come and get him, she's an idiot.''

''If only she'd told me who the father is!'' Holly said. ''Maybe he knows where she went.''

''Yes, well, it's your wedding day, Holly Jeannette Rivers-almost-Samuelson, so let's forget Jazz, for once.'' Lifting a circlet of flowers, Alice placed it expertly atop Holly's thick hair. A gauzy veil turned the world blurry until the salon owner tipped it upward. "It's hinged, thank goodness. So you don't have to stumble around until your final march."

"You make that sound like the march of doom!" Yielding her nephew to Alice, Holly picked up her bouquet. The tightly bound flowers had a light, refreshing smell.

"Oh, I like Trevor," said her friend. "I just think he's too old for you. And too much like a familiar pair of shoes. Where's your romantic spirit? Don't you want to meet someone exciting?"

"Apparently my sister met someone exciting, and a lot of good it did her!" Holly rejoined. "Oh, Alice, I miss her so much. What if something bad's happened to her? She's so talented, so intense—"

"And so unreliable," her employer pointed out as she retrieved a bottle of formula from the diaper bag. "Any day now, she'll breeze back as if she'd never been away."

"I hope so."

The older woman settled onto a chair and positioned the baby for feeding. "Why don't you get a breath of fresh air? Just make sure Trevor isn't lurking around stealing glances at his bride."

"I think *that's* romantic," Holly returned. "He loves me, Alice. He may be an old friend, but he's got all the qualities of an ideal husband."

"Rich, handsome and boring." Her friend sniffed.

Suddenly Holly *did* need a breath of fresh air. Anyway, it was obvious her friend wanted to be alone with the baby.

"I'll be right back," she said, and went out through a short hallway into the courtyard. It separated the

Sunday school building, which housed her dressing room, from the Spanish-style stucco chapel.

The air was January-crisp, with thin sunshine straggling through the clouds. Last night's drizzle had darkened the high stucco wall that blocked her view of the street.

In back, an alley separated the chapel courtyard from a vacant lot filled with wildflowers. In the courtyard, the flowers were more refined: rose-colored camellias, pale pink azaleas and white calla lilies. Still, the predominant fragrance was wet earth.

As usual when she was alone, Holly's thoughts returned to her sister. People said the two of them looked alike, but she knew better. Jazz was more dramatic in every way: two inches taller, with brighter red hair, darker brown eyes and a more vivacious manner.

Abruptly, she realized she was being watched. Startled, she stared at the man standing across the alley. Where had he come from? The fact that she hadn't seen or heard him approach gave her a creepy sensation.

He stood motionless, regarding her the way a cat watches its prey. Tall and dark, with a short beard and mustache, he had a muscular build beneath his sweatshirt and jeans. He wore a California Angels baseball cap, turned backward.

The most striking thing about the man was the intensity of the eyes. They burned at her from his chiseled face, disturbing her with their open expression of dislike.

Annoyed, Holly reached up and lowered her veil. Not a twitch of the stranger's lips betrayed a reaction.

She hurried inside, but an impression of alert tension stayed with her. And of fierce eyes that seemed oddly familiar.

"YOU ARE certain it is she?" asked Zahad. To Sharif, the turtleneck sweater and cap gave his cousin a collegiate air.

"She covered her face when she saw me, but yes," the sheikh replied. "I am certain." The resemblance to the photograph of H. J. Rivers was unmistakable.

The two men sat in the front seat of a rented sedan, next to a small shopping center on the far side of the vacant lot. Through binoculars, they had been watching the churchyard for more than an hour.

Although, following Zahad's advice, the sheikh was dressed in casual American fashion, something about him had distressed Holly Rivers. He should not have stared so hard, he supposed, but he had wanted to see her face clearly.

How innocent she looked, and how lovely, her youth and vivid coloring flattered by the ivory gown. He knew her true nature, however. She had stolen his money, and now she was trying to steal his child.

"They are all snakes," he muttered. "Her, and those people at the clinic."

Beside him, Zahad nodded. "I am sorry I steered you to that place. It received many recommendations on the Internet, so I trusted Mrs. Wheaton, but she has deceived us. I am only glad we had not yet paid her the full amount."

A month ago, the clinic owner had stopped returning Zahad's phone calls. When he finally reached her, she had nervously declared that there were some unforeseen complications but that they could be handled. Any precipitous action might create legal problems, she had said.

With his usual thoroughness, the aide had checked recent legal records concerning H. J. Rivers. That was how he'd learned that Holly Jeannette Rivers had taken out a marriage license with Trevor Samuelson, an attorney.

Amy Haroun, who had grown up as more of a sister to Sharif than a cousin, had surmised that Holly Rivers must have decided to keep the baby. A poor manicurist couldn't afford a legal battle, but marriage to an attorney would guarantee her an inside track. No doubt the older man had been bedazzled by this manipulative young woman.

Zahad had flown to America at once. Sharif, who'd arrived yesterday, didn't know the full extent of his aide's preparations, but there was a safe house, and this car had been rented through a business subsidiary. Zahad had also stashed a backup vehicle somewhere.

They had brought no weapons, at the sheikh's orders. He didn't want to risk being arrested with a gun.

The plan was to snatch his son and fly him back to Alqedar, using any of several sets of tickets purchased from different airlines. Then let Holly Jeannette Rivers twist and scheme as she might. American custody orders were not recognized in his country.

It had not been easy to catch Ms. Rivers alone with the baby, however. That short woman, who must be her older sister, seemed to be with her whenever the fiancé was absent.

But they had to make their move soon. The Rivers woman had seen him. Even if she didn't already suspect Sharif's identity, any further sightings of him would raise the alarm.

Adrenaline surged through him. Despite the gravity of the situation, this was the moment when he felt most alive: on the verge of action.

"Let us take our positions," said Zahad.

The sheikh nodded. His palms itched and sheer energy pumped through his arteries. To strike at last, after so much delay, would be a pleasure.

INSIDE HER dressing room, Holly found the baby watching wide-eyed as Alice mopped a white milky stain from the shoulder of her blue dress. "The receiving blanket slipped while I was burping him. What a mess!"

"I'll take him." After pushing up her veil, Holly reached for the warm bundle. "You go put some soap and water on it."

"How could I be so clumsy?" fussed her friend as she hurried away.

In Holly's arms, Ben yawned, ready for a nap. She decided to go in search of Marta Vasquez, the salon's other manicurist, who had volunteered to hold the baby during the ceremony.

When she stepped through the outer door, a sharp breeze tugged at her veil. With her bouquet tucked in the crook of her arm and Ben in the other, she didn't have a hand free to steady the veil.

She forgot about the wind, however, when the baby gurgled happily. Holly beamed down at his small pink face.

A scuffing noise, very close, startled her into looking up. It was the dark-haired man. Right there, towering over her, so close she could see the hard purpose in his face.

"Wh-what do you want?" The words came out in a whisper.

She hadn't realized anyone else was present until, from the other side, a pair of hands seized Ben. The second attacker frightened her even more. His marked face and cold expression were terrifying.

Things were happening too fast. It took forever to reach out for little Ben, and when she did, he had already been snatched out of reach. She tried to scream for help, but her throat clamped down.

Where was everybody? Why didn't Trevor come? What did these men want with her baby?

They turned to flee. With a sob, Holly leaped after them.

## *Chapter Two*

The sheikh had thought himself prepared for any development. But he had not anticipated that this woman would throw herself into the car through its half-open rear door when it was already beginning to move.

"Push her out!" cried Zahad, who had thrust the baby into a basket on the floor, and was stepping on the gas. "Close the door!"

The veil and attached circlet of flowers fell to the pavement as the woman clutched at Sharif. "Give me my baby! Give him back!"

"We will not harm him!" Didn't she realize who they must be? "Zahad, stop and let me remove her."

"No!" The woman held fast to Sharif's arm. "I won't leave him!"

"You must close the door!" said his aide. "We are attracting attention, and I cannot drive properly."

As a veteran of many battles, the sheikh would not hesitate to attack a foe. He saw no justification, however, for shoving Holly Rivers from a moving car.

Instead, he yanked her onto the seat beside him, reached past her and slammed the door. Immediately, his cousin whipped onto a street to their right. He swerved again, setting a complicated course in case of pursuit.

As the woman beside him straightened herself, Sharif got a better look at her face. The amber eyes were wide with alarm, and the dishevelled red hair tumbled around her shoulders as if she had newly arisen from bed.

A stunning woman. In spite of himself, he could not help wishing she were his.

Perhaps he had been unfair. In his anger, Sharif realized, he had not considered how strong the surrogate's attachment to the infant might be. Under other circumstances, such mother love would be admirable.

"We do not intend to harm you," he said. "We can release you here if you like."

The woman ignored the offer. "What do you want, a ransom?" Her voice trembled. "I don't have any money but my fiancé does."

"You think we are kidnappers?" She had no sense at all. "You insult us!"

"In a sense, you must admit, we *are* kidnappers," Zahad said with his usual maddening exactitude.

"You exaggerate!" Sharif returned.

"It is a point of fact," his cousin replied, and snapped the sedan around another corner so abruptly that the surrogate fell onto the sheikh's lap.

It had been a long time since Sharif held a woman in his arms. Perhaps this long abstinence explained why he found himself so keenly aware of every soft curve pressed against his body. Of the pulse of Holly's throat, and the sound of her breathing, and the light sweet scent of her.

He reminded himself that this woman had cheated

him and still posed a threat to his people's future. And to his right to share his son's life.

"Let me go!" she gasped.

"I am not restraining you," Sharif replied.

Scrambling onto the seat, she said, "Of course you're restraining me! You're holding my child hostage!"

"Hostage?" He raised an eyebrow. "You should not be surprised that I expect you to make good on your bargain."

"What bargain?" She scooted as far from him as the space allowed. "No bargain gives you the right to assault me at my wedding and snatch Ben! Where have you put him?"

"The baby is in a basket on the floor beside me," Zahad said. "He is smiling. I think he will like to drive fast when he grows up."

"He should be in a car seat!" Holly said. "It's the law!"

Her outrage startled a chuckle from Sharif. The woman certainly had spirit! "And you have observed that we are great devotees of the law?"

From her tightened fists, he got the impression she would like to teach him respect, for the law and for a few other things as well. What a splendid bride she would make for a desert warrior! But not for him.

As Zahad slowed, the sheikh saw that they had reached a broad thoroughfare. Without stopping for the red light, he turned right and accelerated ahead of a bus.

Holly flinched. "You're going to get us killed! There's a reason why you're supposed to stop for red lights, even if you don't care about the law!"

"As a point of fact, we do care about the law,"

said Sharif. "And about civil contracts. It is unfortunate your concern does not extend to those."

"Contracts?" She blinked at him. "What are you talking about?" Some of the fight evaporated from her bunched muscles. "Does Jazz owe you money?"

"Who is Jazz?" he asked.

"My sister."

He remembered the stocky woman at the church. "I know nothing of your sister."

The woman swallowed. "You haven't hurt her?"

This conversation made no sense. The sister had not even come outside, so how could he have hurt her? "Of course not."

"Then—then you're not in any real trouble yet. Just give me the baby and let us go." Tears glittered in Holly's eyes. With her full lips parted, she looked vulnerable and very desirable.

She was a fool if she believed he would part with his son because of a woman's tears. "You are wasting your breath."

"Get down!" shouted Zahad, and the car veered. Without waiting for an explanation, the sheikh grabbed Holly and flattened them both on the seat.

The left-hand passenger window exploded. Bits of glass sprayed across the exposed skin of Sharif's neck.

"The boy?" he demanded. "Is he hurt?"

"He is fine," his cousin said.

"Someone's shooting at us?" Judging by the pitch of her voice, Holly Rivers teetered on the edge of hysteria.

He doubted the police would be so reckless, with a woman and child in the car. "Perhaps this is how your groom thinks to reclaim you."

"Trevor wouldn't do that!"

"I agree, it is not him." Zahad sped through traffic. "The attorney drives a new Cadillac. We are being chased by an old sedan with dark windows."

"It seems my enemies have tracked us," Sharif muttered.

"What enemies?" Holly was shaking. "Who are you guys, anyway?"

It was an odd question for a woman who had agreed of her own free will to bear his child. "We will discuss that later," said Sharif. "By then, I think the answer will come to you."

A series of furious zigzags climaxed in a swift ascent and rapid acceleration. They had entered the freeway.

Zahad checked his rearview mirror. "Our pursuers are dropping back. There is a highway patrol car... They have turned back."

Cautiously, Sharif helped Holly sit up. "How is the baby now?"

"Sleeping," said his cousin.

A moment later, he discovered that he should not have taken his attention from the woman. The combination of a shattered window and an approaching highway patrol car proved irresistible.

"Help!" she screamed, leaning out. "I've been kidnapped!"

The wind tore away her words. From his pocket, Sharif pulled a dampened cloth that Zahad had provided for such an emergency.

Clamping it over the woman's face, he hauled her back into the car. She struggled briefly, then sagged.

When he was certain she slept, Sharif removed the cloth. Although his cousin had promised the dose was not harmful, he was relieved to hear her steady if shallow breathing. A check of the patrol car showed that it had surged ahead in the fast lane, paying them no attention.

"I will pull over at the next exit," Zahad said. "We must leave her."

"Lying by the road, unconscious?" The sheikh shook his head. "Not unless we can find a hospital."

"So you will walk in there and say, 'Excuse me, please take this woman, goodbye?'" His cousin grimaced in the rearview mirror. "We have problems, my friend, and we do not need to add to them."

"We have no problems that will not be solved by flying home," Sharif said.

His cousin passed a slow-moving panel truck. "Think, my friend. Maimun's surviving zealots are not stupid. They found us near the church. That means perhaps they can find us again."

Reluctantly, Sharif conceded the point. "They must have learned of Ms. Rivers's marriage, as we did. So they know about her, and therefore about my son."

"Someone has been tracking our comings and goings," his aide said. "Possibly an employee of the airlines or the airport in Alqedar. They must have tracked me on my last visit here."

"Then they also know of our return reservations." Sharif shook his head, impatient with these obstacles. "So we simply take a circuitous route. Fly from Los Angeles to, say, London. Then to Riyadh…"

Zahad grimaced. "I advise that we do our homework first. We have no idea how many of them there are, or how well-placed. We need more information before we dare to appear in public."

Sharif started to argue. But he knew his cousin was right. They were stuck here, at least for a while.

Another thought hit him. "Then we must keep Ms. Rivers in our custody until we leave. Otherwise, she would give the police too much information."

"Unfortunately, you are right." Zahad punched the radio controls. "Let us see if we have yet made the news reports."

As they listened to sports headlines, Holly snuggled against Sharif's shoulder. The scent of flowers clung to her, along with a trace of baby powder. She seemed less a woman than a nymph, dozing in a cloud of red hair.

A newscaster's voice broke through the sheikh's thoughts. "Police in Harbor View say a bride has been kidnapped moments before her wedding. This happened less than fifteen minutes ago outside the First Community Harbor View Church."

"They are quick with their news," Zahad observed.

"The police no doubt want the public to watch for us," Sharif said.

"The woman, whose identity is being withheld, has collar-length auburn hair and is wearing an ivory wedding gown," said the announcer. "A witness reported seeing her forced into a tan car driven by two men with dark hair and short beards. We'll keep you posted as this story develops."

When a commercial came on, Zahad smacked the steering wheel. "What witness? I saw no one! Americans are too nosy."

"We made a spectacle of ourselves, as I recall," the sheikh said. "Well, we will need to change our appearance as soon as we reach the safe house."

"That is so." Zahad drove for a time in silence.

Sharif wondered if, once Holly awoke, he could persuade her to admit that he was entitled to his son. Perhaps, in exchange for her immediate release, she would help them settle the matter with the police.

Then he could focus on the would-be assassins. And on forgetting a clear-eyed woman with fiery hair and flower-scented skin.

On the radio, the announcer returned. "Here's an update on that kidnapping of a bride in Harbor View. Apparently her three-month-old nephew was also abducted. Police are already investigating the earlier disappearance of the child's mother."

A cold chill swept over Sharif. Holly Jeannette Rivers wasn't the mother of his child. He had taken the wrong woman.

HOLLY'S HEAD felt as if someone had stuffed it with wool, and her wrists chafed. Through the thin mattress, springs and crossbars dug into her back.

She struggled to connect the scattered images in her brain. Alice and the flowers. Trevor, giving her that familiar lopsided grin. The church courtyard, with clouds gathering overhead.

A man stood in the alley, his hands thrust in pockets set into the front of his sweatshirt. Despite his jeans and baseball cap, his beard and his intensity made him seem foreign.

And then—a madly swerving car. And the man, holding her.

The hardness of his body had imprinted itself on her memory. In his grip, she'd felt a reluctant stirring of something she didn't want to name. Something she'd never felt for Trevor.

Then had come the shock of being yanked onto the seat. Had she hit her head? Had she been shot? Anguished, she tried to force herself awake, but her eyelids stuck.

She felt the bite of winter air, tinged with waves of warmth and laced with the aroma of burning wood. Not far off, a low voice murmured in a language she didn't understand.

Then something erased all other perceptions. It was the sound of Ben gurgling and cooing.

Frustrated, Holly tried to sit up, and discovered that her hands and feet were tied. When she managed to open her eyes, moisture blurred her vision until she blinked twice to clear it.

Her first impression was of a rustic cabin. She lay on a fold-out couch in an alcove, beyond which she could see a wood-paneled room with blinds on the windows. A table lamp was augmented by the flickering of an unseen fire.

She inched along the mattress until a large stone fireplace came into view. On a small table nearby, a blanket had been spread. Atop it lay the tiny figure of Ben, his arms waving.

One glimpse of the man towering over him made Holly go rigid.

Although the beard and mustache were gone, the piercing gaze belonged unmistakably to the man who had attacked her in the churchyard. Instead of jeans, he wore a white headdress and robe that made him look utterly alien.

Her first, confused reaction was that a sheikh had ridden out of some old movie. Reality was much more terrifying. The man who had her and Ben at his mercy must be some kind of delusional maniac.

She prayed that he wouldn't notice she was awake. Surely she could find a way to untie her hands and rescue her nephew.

Holly studied the cord binding her. There was no slack, and no apparent weakness in the rope, either.

Cautiously, she twisted her wrists. The cord bit harder. Holly pressed her lips together to keep from crying out.

Her captor paid her no attention. But he must be doing something that Ben didn't like, because the baby began squalling.

"Don't hurt him!" she called. "If you have to torture someone, do it to me!"

The dark man looked up, and she noticed a white object in his hand. A diaper. For heaven's sake, he was trying to change the baby!

If Holly hadn't been so frightened, she might have found his expression comical. It was the kind of befuddled expression Trevor had worn once when she thrust Ben into his arms so she could answer a phone call.

"So, you are awake," he said. "I am sorry I was forced to drug you. Do you have any pain?"

"I'm just...sleepy." Her voice sounded hollow. "What time is it?"

"A little past seven."

Holly groaned. Her wedding was ruined. The guests, Trevor, Alice. What must they think?

"Believe me, I have no intention of torturing anyone." Her captor indicated her ties. "The sooner I can return you to your bridegroom, the better, but in the meantime certain precautions were regrettably necessary."

Holly had to admit that, clean-shaven, his face was

handsome in a thoroughly masculine way, and his expression not unkind. But what about the outlandish costume?

"Why are you wearing that?" she asked.

He smoothed down his robe. "I would not go outside dressed this way, not in your country. But I wanted my son to see me as I really am."

"Your—?" She didn't need to finish the question. Not when she'd finally realized why those penetrating eyes looked so familiar.

They were Ben's eyes.

"You're his father," she whispered. "Oh, Lord." Through the lingering effects of medication, her brain churned over this disturbing discovery. She'd found Jazz's secret lover, or, rather, he'd found her and Ben. "What have you done with my sister?"

The man returned his attention to the baby. "Nothing. I thought you were her."

"What?" Holly made the mistake of trying to push herself up. The cords tightened again, making her wince. "How could you?"

"I know her only from a photograph. It was arranged through a clinic. She did not tell you?" He put one hand beneath the baby's backside and tried to raise his bottom while sliding the diaper beneath it.

Free-spirited Jazz would never have agreed to bear this child for pay! "I don't believe you. Why would my sister want to be a surrogate mother?"

"I was told she wanted money to make a demonstration recording." He broke off as Ben kicked lustily, flinging one of his booties into a corner and dislodging the diaper from the man's grip.

"You're doing that wrong!"

"Evidently." Keeping one hand on the baby, the man leaned back and squinted at the child. "It appears to be a problem of structural engineering."

"You're an engineer?" Holly needed to make sense of this situation, and to learn anything she could.

"I am many things," the man replied enigmatically. "But I am not an abuser of women. I will release you from your bonds if you will care for my son. As you have pointed out, I don't seem to be doing very well at it."

His accent sounded Middle Eastern. "Where are you from?"

"Your sister told you nothing of me?" Wrapping the fussing baby in the blanket, he carried him, along with the diaper, to Holly.

"Nothing at all. And believe me, I tried to find out who the father was." She started to reach for Ben, and stopped with a gasp.

The man set the baby on the center of the bed. "My cousin Zahad must have tied the rope too tightly. He was in a hurry."

At close range, she could see small cuts on the man's neck from where shards of glass had hit him. Other than that, his skin had a smooth olive cast, with some roughness where he'd recently shaved.

The man smelled of shampoo, and his thick hair, what she could see of it, was damp, so he must have showered since they arrived. Yet there was an undercurrent of wild musk about him that no soap could wash away.

From inside the robe flashed a knife. Holly scarcely had time to register the danger before the man sliced the cord between her wrists, then the one at her ankles. The knife disappeared into the folds of cloth.

Prickles of agonizing sensation shot through her hands and feet. "Your cousin—that would be the driver? Is he here?"

"He thought it best to stay in a different place." The bed dipped as the man sat beside her. With a shiver, Holly saw the smoldering fire in his gaze as he watched her. "Although this canyon is remote, if he and I were seen together, it might draw suspicion."

"You mean from the police?" Although her captor spoke calmly, she reminded herself that law-abiding men didn't go around snatching brides and babies.

"Yes. Among others." Before she could query further, the man said, "I don't think it is good for the boy to lie here in only his little shirt. Do you know how to put on a diaper?"

"I should hope so." She flexed her stinging limbs. "But it might take me a minute to get full sensation back in my hands. Thanks to your overeager cousin."

"He takes pride in his thoroughness," the man said.

"He should take a little more pride in showing consideration for others!" she flared.

Her captor smiled. Pure white teeth gleamed against his tanned skin. "You sound like my cousin Amy. She finds fault with Zahad also."

The prickly sensations eased. Skillfully, Holly caught the baby's ankles in her left hand, hoisted up his bottom and slid the diaper into place. Ben chuckled and reached for her.

"Amazing," said the man in the sheikh's robe. "You do that with such ease. And he is clearly attached to you."

"He knows I love him." Holly cradled the baby in her arms.

The man watched them, his expression unreadable. "I, too, love him."

"How can you, when you don't even know him?"

"And you think you do?" The man unfolded himself from the bed and began to pace, his restless energy filling the room. "What do you know of this boy's history? Of his heritage or his future? To you, he is a tiny baby, but someday he will be a great man!"

"He'll be whatever he wants to be. You can't force a child to meet someone else's expectations." Holly held Ben close. There no longer seemed to be any point in safeguarding her wedding dress, which was thoroughly rumpled and flecked with blood from Sharif's injuries.

"Your sister understood my son's importance, according to the clinic's director," said her companion.

"The clinic," she repeated. "This is so unlike Jazz."

"Jazz?"

"My sister. It's short for Hannah Jasmine," she said. "We've called her that since she was a kid. She hated going to the doctor. And she wasn't even close to what you might call maternal."

Outside, something thwacked against a window. Holly's heart skittered into her throat.

Moving quickly and silently, her captor switched off the lamp. As its circular glow faded, scarlet firelight crept eerily across the walls.

"Lie down!" the man whispered as he edged toward the window.

Holly obeyed, shielding Ben with her body. Had

the people who'd fired at their car found the cabin as well? Or could it be the police?

The scraping noise returned, following by a pattering on the roof. Her captor lifted a slat of blinds and peered into the night.

Finally, he turned the lamp back on. "It was a branch in the wind. The rain has started, as you can hear. It should be quite a storm."

Holly swallowed her disappointment. She had hoped it was the police coming to rescue her and Ben. But at least it wasn't armed assailants, either.

"Who shot at us earlier?" she asked. "And who are you? I don't even know your name."

The man drew himself up proudly. Somehow his confident air made his robe and headdress appear less outlandish. In fact, Holly could have sworn they suited him better than the jeans and sweatshirt he'd worn that afternoon.

"I am Sheikh Sharif Al-Khalil of Alqedar." He delivered this bizarre information without a trace of self-consciousness. "That is a small nation in south-central Arabia, in case you do not know. Although my son has been born in America, I have every right to take him home."

The words "sheikh" and "Arabia" seemed like phrases from a fairy tale. "Who are you really?"

An eyebrow lifted, and then he laughed. "You do not believe me? I'm not surprised. But it is true."

She tried a different tack. "Ben was born here. That makes him a U.S. citizen. You can't just whisk him off, not if his mother opposes it."

The man shrugged. "It seems that his mother has found better ways to occupy her time."

"I'm his next closest relative!"

"And you would have married yourself a lawyer to defend your so-called rights," he observed with a trace of sarcasm. "How very American of you."

Although the implication infuriated Holly, she wouldn't stoop to debate it. "What's between Trevor and me is none of your business. And even if you are a sheikh and Ben really is your son, nothing gives you the right to hold me prisoner!"

"You chose to jump in the car with us. That was your decision." The man regarded her with what might have been sympathy, or merely irony. "I am afraid I cannot let you go yet, Ms. Rivers, even though it was to be your wedding night. Perhaps I can make it up to you."

Her throat tightened.

He regarded her with amusement. "I did not mean that literally, but it could be arranged."

He was a sheikh, but more importantly, he was a leader from a foreign country. If he possessed diplomatic immunity, Holly thought in a burst of fear, he could do anything he wanted, and get away with it.

# *Chapter Three*

Sharif did not understand why, after all these years, he was suddenly seized with the desire to possess a woman. Why at this perilous time, when he needed to stay alert, and why this defiant woman?

From the moment he'd held her in the car, Holly had aroused a response like no woman since Yona. And now, in the rise and fall of her breasts as she stared at him, he read a rising passion that matched his own.

She was fighting her desire in vain. He knew from his younger days what it took to seduce a woman, and this one lay within his power. All it would take was the touch of his lips against her face and throat, and the hard commanding movements of his body, and he could bring them both to ecstasy.

Holly's eyes widened. With fear or longing, or both? "Don't," she whispered. "Please."

She was, the sheikh reminded himself sharply, another man's bride. She was also a threat to his ability to take his son back to Alqedar.

Stiffly, he drew back. "You have nothing to fear. I told you, I am not an abuser of women."

"And you really don't know what's happened to

my sister?'' Even at this tense moment, Holly Rivers was more concerned for the missing woman than for herself, he saw with reluctant admiration.

''I wish I did.'' Sharif bent and ran one finger along his son's cheek. ''It would be easier to straighten out this mess if she were here. Unless she intended, as I feared, to seek custody.''

''I don't know what she intended.'' The young woman brushed back a wave of red hair that had fallen across her temple. ''I haven't seen her in three months, since before Ben was born.''

''Then how did you get him?''

''A friend of hers brought him, a musician named Griff Goldbar. He said she would come back in a few days. That was over a month ago.''

About that time, the clinic owner had stopped taking Zahad's calls. Such a coincidence must be meaningful. ''Do you know a woman named Noreen Wheaton?''

''No, why?''

''She's the head of the clinic that hired your sister,'' he said. ''If you've been searching for Jasmine, surely you found some record of the surrogacy arrangement.''

Holly's expression grew troubled. ''Jazz must have taken her contract with her. I cleaned out her room, but there weren't any papers from a clinic.'' The baby began to squirm. ''I think he's hungry.''

''I'll get the formula.'' Sharif went to fetch the bag that Aunt Selima had packed.

As he crossed the cabin, he wondered why the clinic director had been reluctant to talk to Zahad. Had there been threats against the clinic and, if so, from whom? With the police after him, Sharif could hardly contact Mrs. Wheaton to ask her directly.

Or perhaps he was looking in the wrong direction. The woman, Jasmine, might have enemies of her own. Her disappearance might bear no relationship to Sharif or to the clinic.

On his way back to the alcove, he tuned the television set to an all-news station, grateful that, in California, even remote cabins came equipped with TV service. At the moment, however, the report concerned local politics.

"My great-aunt provided these supplies." He set the bag beside Holly on the bed. "She and my cousin Amy will care for the child when I get home."

"You're not married?" In the filtered light, the woman could have passed for a teenager.

"My wife died many years ago." To cut off further questions, he presented her with a can of formula. "Is it necessary to heat it?"

"Not really," Holly said. "Do you have a clean bottle?"

"I would scarcely bring a dirty one!" He handed it to her. "How long will that last?"

"There's enough for two feedings, so maybe half a day. Is this all you've got?"

"There are two more cans." Obviously, it would not be enough. "Zahad will get more."

After filling the bottle, the woman settled the baby at the same angle Selima had demonstrated. Sharif wondered whether women did these things by instinct, but he knew better than to ask an American woman.

"You have a phone?" she said.

Sharif patted his robe.

"I wondered if I could call my fiancé," she said. "Trevor must be going crazy."

Trevor. Ah, yes, the athletic blond man in his forties who had crossed the courtyard that afternoon. Sharif no longer believed Holly had manipulated her groom, yet she didn't speak of him as if she were in love. Her reasons for marrying were, however, none of his business.

"I am sorry to put you both to this inconvenience," he said. "However, the police will be monitoring his telephone and might be able to locate us."

"Even through a cell phone?"

"It is possible," he said. "The technology is developing rapidly."

From the TV, the word "kidnapping" drew his attention. A picture came on screen, a blurry angled shot taken from overhead. It showed Sharif, Zahad and Holly getting into the car.

"A security camera in a strip mall captured this scene earlier today in Harbor View, where a bride and her nephew were abducted minutes before her wedding," said a woman announcer's voice.

"The victim has been identified as Holly Jeannette Rivers, a hairstylist from Harbor View. Her sister, Hannah Jasmine Rivers, vanished three months ago. Hannah Rivers is the mother of the kidnapped baby."

A security camera! Sharif cursed under his breath. Neither he nor Zahad had considered that possibility in such a small row of stores.

The picture changed to computer-enhanced close-ups of Sharif's and Zahad's faces, side by side, like a wanted poster. He realized the camera must have taken numerous shots during their hour-long surveillance.

"Police say the men in the photograph have been tentatively identified as Sheikh Sharif Al-Khalil and his aide, Zahad Adran, from the small Arabian nation of Alqedar."

How? he wondered, and then realized the camera must also have captured the license plate on the rental car, which could be traced to a subsidiary of the Bahrim Corporation. With that information and those pictures, it wouldn't take long to make an ID.

"A spokesman for the State Department told our station that the sheikh is not in the country on official business and has no diplomatic immunity," the announcer said. "It is unclear what connection he has with the Rivers family."

Sharif had known he ran a security risk four years ago when he relinquished his powerful post in the central government to devote himself to the well-being of his province, but he had never anticipated such a situation as this.

Alqedar's president, Sheikh Abdul Dourad, was an old friend. In his fifties, the president had fought for freedom alongside Sharif and Zahad. However, even he could not retroactively grant diplomatic immunity.

On TV, the anchorwoman sat at her desk beside a blond man in a business suit. "We have with us Trevor Samuelson, the fiancé of kidnap victim Holly Rivers." She turned to him. "Mr. Samuelson is an attorney in Harbor View and would like to say a few words to the abductors."

"Just don't hurt Holly or Ben." The man stared into the camera. "Whatever your quarrel is, if you want money or whatever, we can work this out."

His expression was earnest but restrained. Like a soldier stoically facing battle, Sharif thought.

"Thank you, Mr. Samuelson. Now for a look at how long this rain is going to last and how much accumulation we can expect…"

Holly wore a guarded expression as she fed the baby. During Trevor's appeal, she'd showed no sign of longing for her betrothed. What *was* she thinking?

And why did she keep sneaking sideways glances at Sharif? Did she too feel this urge to touch?

Her tenderness toward his son formed a bond between them. A man and woman who shared a baby usually also shared the intimacy of their bodies. But she was not the mother, the sheikh reminded himself. And she was not, and never could be, his woman.

The mobile phone rang. After muting the TV, he answered it.

Zahad spoke in Baharalik, an ancient language that survived only in Bahrim. "Did you see the newscast? Yes? I am angry with myself. I should have spotted the camera."

"We may still be able to resolve this matter," Sharif said. "Since the mother is missing, I doubt we face a custody battle."

"Only charges of kidnapping!"

Holding the baby against a cloth laid over her shoulder, Holly was rubbing his back with circular motions. She appeared to pay him no notice.

Into the phone, he said, "I hope to persuade the woman to drop charges. She has accepted that I am the child's father, and she did leap into the car of her own free will."

"I doubt she or the authorities will see it that way," grumbled his cousin. "I do not think it wise to trust her."

Zahad was a genius at intrigues, but sometimes,

Sharif had learned, the shortest distance between two points really was a straight line. "Nevertheless, we need to get my son home quickly. If I can persuade her to plead our cause, it might help."

"She will lie to you," warned his aide.

"Perhaps," he conceded. "I will have to use my judgment."

"I would rather you used your wits," Zahad said. "Although, I admit, you have reason to doubt my advice, now that we have been shot at and photographed all in one day."

"I do not doubt you," Sharif said. "You are my other self."

"As you are mine. I will call as soon as I learn anything from my sources in Alqedar. So far, they have uncovered no rumors of a plot."

The sheikh rang off with a silent prayer of thanks for his faithful relative. Although they had attended different universities while exiled during their country's dictatorship, they had trained together at a military camp, and they had both shed blood in the war of liberation. There was no one he trusted more than Zahad.

Perhaps the man was right about Holly. Perhaps she would lie in order to liberate herself, then betray him. But he had to try to win her over, for his son's sake.

HOLLY WISHED she were an expert at languages. If only she knew what the men had been saying!

At least, according to the newscast, Sharif had told the truth about his identity. He really was a sheikh, and he'd given her his true name.

Did that mean he was being honest about Jazz?

That he hadn't harmed her, and that her sister really had become a surrogate to raise money for a demo recording?

It was, Holly supposed, the kind of impulsive scheme that Jazz might get involved in. But surely Sharif knew more than he was telling about her sister's disappearance.

She bit her lip. Nothing in her quiet life had prepared her to deal with this brooding, complicated man.

At least the effects of the medication had worn off. She felt tired and sore, but her brain was functioning.

"You must be hungry." Lamplight etched shadows into the man's face.

"I guess so." She tried not to think about Trevor and the wedding reception he'd planned at his favorite restaurant.

In the corner kitchenette, the sheikh opened a refrigerator. His broad shoulders blocked Holly's view of the contents.

At last he swung around. "We have plenty to eat, if you like Middle Eastern food."

"That's fine." Holly had eaten at several exotic restaurants with Trevor, although she couldn't remember much about the food. "Do you know how to cook?"

"Only over a campfire." The sheikh removed a platter. "Fortunately, this can be microwaved."

A sense of unreality teased at Holly. Was she really about to eat dinner with an Arabian sheikh in a robe and headdress?

As he moved around the kitchen, the white fabric molded itself to his powerful build. She wished she weren't so aware of Sharif's leashed strength and the smoldering way he studied her when he thought she was unaware.

For one traitorous moment, she wished that, for one night, she could be someone other than prosaic Holly Rivers. That she could yield to instincts that she didn't understand and couldn't possibly justify.

No, she must not think that way. She must set her mind to escaping.

The man had said they were in a canyon. Even in paved-over Orange County, there remained wilderness areas with thick undergrowth inhabited by coyotes and mountain lions. Did she really dare to take the baby out there?

Gazing down at Ben, Holly saw that he'd dozed off. Gently, she settled him on the center of the queen-size bed.

The bell on the microwave indicated their food was ready. Her mind still mulling the dangers of an escape, Holly stood up. Without warning, the world began to spin, and she groped shakily for support.

Swiftly, Sharif reached her side. As he caught Holly's arm, her knees went weak and she had to lean against him.

"The drug must be affecting your balance," he said. "It will help if you eat something."

"I thought I was over it." Glancing up, she found his face close to hers, his gaze filled with concern. She knew she ought to be frightened, but instead she felt relaxed. Trusting.

"Stay in bed. I'll bring the food here." His low tone vibrated through her.

"No." Holly didn't dare fall asleep again. They needed to talk. The more she knew, the better her chances of getting out alive. "I want to sit at the table."

"I'll help you." One arm encircled her waist. As the sheikh steered her across the room, she detected other thicknesses of cloth beneath the white fabric. So he was dressed under his robe. The realization highlighted how little she knew about him or his culture.

"At home, do you live in a tent, or a palace, or what?" she asked. "I don't know much about Alqedar. Or about sheikhs, either."

His jaw worked, and she realized he was suppressing a smile. Okay, she probably *did* sound like an idiot, but how was she to know?

"I live in a palace, and we have all the comforts of home." Supporting her with one arm, he pulled out a chair at the wooden table. "Most of Alqedar's leaders are educated in the West. We must be able to bridge two worlds, preserving our traditions while meeting the industrialized nations on their own terms."

"You certainly speak English well." She sank onto the chair, and immediately missed the comfort of his nearness. "Where did you go to school?"

"At Columbia, in New York." He took a seat opposite her. "So I am familiar with your country."

"New York is only one small part of America."

"I have traveled through most of the states," he said. "The dramatic landscapes of Utah and Arizona are like nothing else I've seen. And some of your cities exert a unique charm."

Holly felt more provincial than ever. She'd seen less of her own country than this foreigner.

He dished some food onto her plate. Inhaling the aromas, Holly found that she really was hungry.

For a while, they ate without speaking. Under the table, the sheikh's legs brushed hers. Although he moved them away, she was left with an impression of muscle and sinew.

"Tell me exactly why you kidnapped Ben," she said. "You were afraid of a custody battle?"

"Exactly. The practices of your legal system do not always tally with those of my country," he said. "We hoped for a quick getaway."

"But now that your plan has failed—"

"It hasn't failed, it has suffered a few setbacks," he replied. "We incurred what you Americans call 'the double whammy.' We got shot twice, first by a camera and then with a gun."

"You never explained who was firing at us," she said. "Do you know?"

"Not for certain." As Sharif ate, she saw that the backs of his hands bore thin, straight scars, as from knife wounds. "I have enemies, from my country's fight for freedom. It is also possible that your sister has enemies."

"Jazz hangs out with some strange people, but as far as I know, they don't carry weapons."

"What kind of strange people?" From a plastic bottle, he poured mineral water into two glasses.

"Musicians." With their long hair and disorderly life-style, Jazz's colleagues had little in common with most people Holly knew. "Maybe they only seem strange in Southern California, because they're more interested in making music than money."

"Your sister was interested in money, to make a demonstration recording," Sharif reminded her.

"I wish she'd told me," Holly said. "I would have loaned it to her. Or Trevor would have. He manages my parents' estate, not that it's worth much. But he's always come through in a pinch. How much did you pay her?''

''A hundred and fifty thousand dollars,'' Sharif said.

She choked on her food, and had to wash it down with water. ''A hundred and—? Jazz got that much?''

''No, only half was paid in advance, and the clinic took a share,'' he said. ''I presume she received something in the order of thirty or forty thousand.''

''She left eleven thousand dollars in her checking account,'' Holly said. ''I'm sure she spent some money on living expenses and maternity clothes. She must have taken the rest with her in cash.''

''And you truly have no idea why she left?''

She shook her head. ''No. I don't know why she sent Ben to me, either.''

''Perhaps that musician friend of hers was involved,'' he said. ''Ten or twenty thousand dollars would be a fortune to him.''

Holly pictured Griff, whom she'd known casually for years. An easygoing, talkative fellow, he played drums in an alternative rock band with which Jazz sang.

He'd had a minor drug conviction a few years back, and he'd managed to avoid being questioned by the police since she reported Jazz missing. Nevertheless, she couldn't imagine him hurting her sister.

''If he were up to something, why would he give himself away by bringing me the baby?'' she pointed out.

The sheikh finished eating. ''I do not know. I am grateful that at least he put my son in good hands.''

Holly's cheeks warmed, and she hurriedly changed

the subject. "I think she left of her own free will, but then something prevented her from coming back for Ben. I've been so worried."

"I share your concern that something has gone wrong," he said slowly. "This Noreen Wheaton, the director of the clinic, might be afraid of someone, or she is playing a game of her own."

He pushed back his chair and walked to a leather suitcase. From a side pocket, he drew some papers. "Here is a copy of our contract with the clinic. I brought it to prove that the baby is mine. Perhaps you will see something in them that I have missed."

The papers bore the name of the Crestline View Clinic. The legal terminology covered such issues as privacy and liability.

Holly studied the signatures at the bottom: Sharif Al-Khalil, witnessed by Zahad Adran, and Noreen Wheaton, witnessed by someone named Manuel Estrellas.

"Do you know anything about this man Estrellas?" she asked.

The sheikh took a seat beside her. "A clinic employee, I presume."

She scanned the contract again. "Why isn't Jazz's name on here?"

"We were told she signed a separate contract with the clinic," Sharif said.

"But she knew about you, right?" Holly returned the document to him. "I mean, that the baby was going to be raised by your aunt and your cousin?"

"You make it sound as if there were something wrong with my arrangements."

Holly plunged in. "I just don't believe Ben will be happy growing up without a mother."

A tightening of the sheikh's mouth indicated that she'd overstepped her bounds. "I would not have arranged to have a son if I could not provide him with a proper home."

Tears pricked Holly's eyes. "I just don't want to lose him."

His harsh expression softened. "Have you considered what will happen when your sister returns?" he said. "By your own account, she is unreliable, and you could not prevent her from reclaiming the child. What kind of life would he lead then?"

"I've been trying not to think about that." Staring down at the table, Holly took a deep breath.

She reminded herself that Trevor wanted to marry her, and there was no reason they couldn't have children of their own. But those children wouldn't be Ben. They wouldn't be the baby who'd opened the floodgates of love inside her.

The sheikh brushed a tear from her cheek. "To lose this child would hurt you very much."

All she could do was nod.

"You are a woman who lives for others," he murmured. "What then is left for yourself?"

"I don't need anything for myself." It seemed so obvious that she was surprised she had to explain it. "What more could a person want than to ensure the happiness of the people she loves?"

His hand cupped her chin. The roughness of his palm testified to a hard life, and yet his fingers stroked her jawline as lightly as a whisper. "Let us reach a sensible agreement, Holly Rivers. One that is truly best for all of us."

"An agreement?" She allowed herself to meet his gaze.

·"I propose that, tomorrow, you and I go together
to the authorities," he said gravely.

"You mean you'll turn yourself in?"

"As soon as I find a lawyer, yes." He studied her.
"Will you promise to explain that you entered my car
of your own free will?"

She nodded. "Of course. It's the truth."

"I will present the contract and show that I have
only taken my own son," he said. "It is a gamble,
but I doubt they will press charges. It would be the
fastest way to resolve this situation. And for us to get
away from whoever is trying to kill me."

"Then what happens to Ben?" Tears threatened
again, because she knew the answer.

"You must admit that he will be better off with
me than with your sister," said the sheikh. "Also, in
compensation for spoiling your wedding, I will pay
for a private detective to search for her."

For a crazy moment, Holly contemplated offering
to go to Alqedar and take care of Ben. Just to keep
him close, this child of her heart. To give him a
mother, after all.

But what place could she have in a land so unfamiliar she doubted she could find it on a map?

Doubts tore at her. What if Sharif was tricking her
in some way? The contract might have been altered.
Maybe nothing was as it seemed to be.

She'd never had to deal with such a situation before. If Trevor were here…but, of course, he wasn't.

She needed this man's trust. And her deepest instincts told her that he would never, under any circumstances, harm Ben.

"All right," she said slowly, still not certain she

was making the right decision. "If everything is as you present it, I agree not to fight for custody."

Outside, the rain settled into a steady, lulling pattern. The long day, the full meal and the lingering effects of medication must be taking their toll, because Holly found herself fighting a yawn.

"You need sleep." Taking her hand, the sheikh pulled her gently to her feet.

At the bed, Holly curled beside Ben. She was only vaguely aware of Sharif tucking the covers around them.

SHE AWOKE to semidarkness and the scents of woodsmoke and baby powder. Rain pattered on the roof while, across the room, the TV glimmered, its sound turned low.

A flash of lightning showed Sharif dozing at the dining table, his head cradled on his arms. Sleep appeared to have caught him unexpectedly.

Beside Holly, the baby murmured and nestled closer. Slowly she began sinking back into slumber.

A quickening in the TV announcer's tone barely penetrated her consciousness until she picked out the words "body" and "woman." The fears of the past few months returned in a flash.

Sliding from the bed, Holly hurried to the set. Cool air nipped her shoulders above the crumpled wedding gown, and the wooden floor chilled her stockinged feet.

"The victim, believed to be in her mid-twenties, was found by off-road bikers in the desert," said the announcer. "Police haven't released her identity."

On the screen, paramedics loaded a blanket-covered body into an ambulance. When they tilted the stretcher, the blanket fell back to reveal a bare arm.

The camera zoomed in on a small tattoo, a botanical cluster of four-petaled blooms.

Holly recognized them at once. They were jasmine flowers.

# Chapter Four

Jazz had come home late one day from high school, proudly displaying the tattoo to which her boyfriend had treated her. It was her namesake, a little bunch of jasmine flowers.

"...appears to have been dead for several weeks," said the announcer.

Several weeks. Holly's head buzzed. If she could believe Griff, Jazz had been alive a month ago and had planned to pick up Ben in a few days.

She must have been killed in the interim. All this time that Holly had been searching, and jumping with fear at every ring of the phone or doorbell, her sister had been lying dead in the desert.

Who had done this? Had Jazz taken up with the wrong set of friends? Had Griff gotten greedy?

There was one other possibility she had to face. That Jazz had purposely sent her son to Holly because she was going to meet the one man who could take him from her.

Sheikh Sharif Al-Khalil.

Holly's throat tightened until she could barely breathe. Could Sharif have done such a thing?

At the table, still in his robe, he lay sleeping harmlessly. Yet she could see the powerful thrust of his shoulders, and the strength in his arms. This was not a man to be trifled with.

She didn't want to believe that the man who had gazed at Ben with such adoration, and treated her with such kindness this evening, might have killed Jazz. He'd spoken so rationally about hiring a lawyer and going to the police tomorrow, that she wanted to believe him.

But a calm facade could hide a lethal temper. Maybe, if crossed, he exploded into an uncontrollable fury.

In Holly's mind burned an image of Jazz's inert body, lying on a stretcher amid the glare of police lights. She'd been cast aside in the desert as if she were nothing. Only one little tattoo announced to the world that this was an individual, a person with friends and dreams of her own.

Through Holly's grief, one point stood out: Her life might be in the same danger as her sister's. Danger rose like woodsmoke, filling the cabin and obscuring every thought except that of flight.

When thunder rumbled, she caught her breath. Would it wake Sharif?

At the table, he muttered softly and shifted position, then stilled. His silence felt like a reprieve.

Gently, she lifted the baby. Since she had no coat, she made a cloak of the bedspread and draped it over them both.

She hated to take the baby into the rain, but she couldn't leave him. If Sharif had a violent temper, he might unleash it on anyone at hand.

To reach the cabin door meant crossing the room. At the moment, it looked as wide as a football field.

Adrenaline and fear powered Holly out of the alcove. One noiseless step followed another.

A board creaked beneath her satin wedding pumps. Holly froze.

The man didn't stir. She moved forward, acutely aware of the weight of the baby in one arm and the swish of fabric audible above the rain. Outside, the wind rose, and a branch scraped the window so loud that it sounded, to her ears, like a bomb blast.

The door. She turned the knob and pulled. It held stubbornly in place.

There had to be a bolt. She just hoped it didn't require a key to open from the inside.

With Ben resting against her shoulder, Holly clamped the bedspread beneath one elbow to keep from dropping it as she probed with her free hand. Was the lock above or below the knob?

*Next time I get kidnapped, I'll make sure to check out the door while there's enough light.*

The grim humor steadied her, and she located a small slide-lock about six inches above the knob. Struggling against the stiff device while trying not the jolt the baby, she tugged on it.

The metal rasped, halted, then slid the rest of the way. Breathing hard, Holly grasped the knob.

Icy wind hit her in the face. Ben squirmed beneath the spread.

Trying to let in as little cold air as possible, she edged outside and closed the door. From beyond a small overhang, rain gusted into her face.

Holly could see nothing except sheets of water and the outline of black trees against a charcoal sky. It was as if she stood on an island surrounded by a raging sea.

A flare of lightning showed her a muddy, unpaved clearing overhung by low branches. A rutted path led away through the brush, with no lights or traffic noises to indicate how close a road might be.

Tightening the makeshift cloak, Holly stepped off the porch into the full force of the storm.

A RAW BLAST of air woke Sharif. He came awake instantly, his warrior's training jolting him to full alert.

The door had opened. Someone had come in or gone out.

Cursing himself for falling asleep on watch, he ducked and dodged in case of attack. Nothing moved, other than a flicker of light from the TV screen. Except for him, the cabin was empty.

The woman had taken his child.

He had promised to deliver her safely to the authorities. She had agreed to tell them the truth. Now she had betrayed that agreement.

He knew better than to assume she was unarmed. Although there were no guns in the cabin, she might have found a knife in a drawer.

A pat of his robe confirmed that the phone was in place, so she hadn't been able to call for help. She wouldn't be able to travel fast on foot, either.

If she blundered into the woods, however, she might easily get lost. A few hours of exposure could prove fatal to the child.

Sharif did not wish to injure Holly. Despite his anger, he couldn't entirely blame her for fleeing. But he must retrieve his son at any cost.

The overriding need to reclaim Ben drove him to

action. He yanked open the door and leaped out, to give the woman no chance to react.

Another long step carried him beyond the porch to the dark cloth-covered shape struggling away from him. Their bodies collided, hard.

In the darkness, Sharif must have misjudged the distance, because he shot way over balance. Grabbing Holly, he managed to twist partway beneath her as they fell, to shield the baby from hitting the ground.

A gasp from the woman blended with the squalling of the bundle in her arms. The impact knocked the breath out of Sharif, but he had no time to waste.

Grasping the child, he rolled away through the mud. Raising himself on one knee, he kept the child tight against him and the woman in sight.

Rain poured over them. The sheikh ignored it as he watched for the flash of a blade.

Instead, he found himself staring into a pair of terrified eyes. From the looks of her, Holly was so frightened she couldn't even scream.

"What on earth are you doing?" he demanded. "I agreed to take you back tomorrow."

Finally, words choked out of her. "You killed her!"

"Who?" Had lingering traces of Zahad's medicine given her a nightmare?

"My sister!"

"I've never even met her. I told you that." He stood up, sheltering the baby beneath his robe. The boy was surprisingly wiggly, and he found it hard to support his head as Aunt Selima had taught. "Besides, for all we know, she is sitting in a bar somewhere, having a laugh at our expense."

"No! How could you…?" As she scrambled to her

feet, Holly still didn't seem capable of finishing a sentence.

"You're not making sense," he told her. "I've been sitting in the cabin all night, not out marauding!"

"She's dead." The pain in her voice convinced him, finally, that she wasn't referring to some dream. "It was on TV."

Sharif had left the set on so he could keep track of what information the police were giving out. "They found your sister?"

Beneath the mud-streaked bedspread that half-covered her, Holly nodded. "In the desert. She's been dead...a few weeks."

Wind whipped the wet tendrils of her hair, giving her a half-drowned appearance. In a flare of lightning, he saw that she was shivering.

"You'll make yourself sick," Sharif said. "Let's continue this conversation inside."

"Let me go. Let us both go!"

"We don't have a car," he pointed out. "Even if I wanted to, I have no way of taking you anywhere on a night like this. And you certainly can't walk out of a canyon in your condition."

Without waiting for a response, he carried the baby up the steps. The woman followed as far as the porch, then stopped in the open doorway.

The best way to reach her, Sharif assessed, was to appeal to her better judgment. Once she examined the facts, surely she would concede that he wasn't guilty, or at least that he might not be.

He sat on the bed and rocked Ben in his arms. It was best to start with the basics, he decided. "Are you certain the murder victim was your sister? Did the police release her identity?''

''I recognized the jasmine flowers on her arm.'' Her teeth chattered when she spoke again. ''There can't be two missing women with the same tattoo.''

So it was true. The mother of his child, the beautiful woman in the photograph, had been killed. Such a waste of a life, he thought.

''I am sorry,'' Sharif said. ''But why should you think I am responsible?''

Holly gathered the bedraggled cloth more tightly around her. ''You had a motive. And contempt for our laws. You've shown me that!''

Despite his irritation at this slur on his honor, Sharif kept his tone steady. ''Laws regarding custody are a matter of culture. Murder is different. To slay a helpless person is a sin against all that is holy.''

''I don't believe you!''

Holly was not a soldier, he reminded himself. She had not been prepared for the death of a loved one, especially on top of the shock of being abducted. ''That is because you don't know me.''

''You didn't have to kill her!'' she persisted. ''My sister wasn't some object who stood between you and your son. You should have heard her sing. And seen how quick she was to laugh. When she was around, the world sparkled.'' Tears flowed down her cheeks. ''Why couldn't you just leave her alone?''

Sharif doubted that mere words would reassure her. She needed something tangible to calm her thoughts.

''Here.'' He took his passport from inside his robe and tossed it to her. ''Catch.''

Holly caught the booklet more by instinct than by intent. ''What's this for?''

"Look at the customs stamps," he said. "I've only been in this country two days. And it has been a long time since my last visit."

Hesitantly, she moved across the threshold into the light and opened the passport. After a minute, she said, "Well, okay, but you could have sneaked in a month ago. Or used a false ID. Or you could have sent Zahad to do your dirty work."

"I could have, but I didn't," he said. "I assure you that if my cousin had located your sister, he would have informed me before taking any action. Now could I have my passport back, please? And would you help me with Ben? He's wet and hungry."

The passport came flying back, but otherwise Holly didn't stir. As she wrapped her arms around herself, she looked like a waif who'd stumbled out of the storm.

At the sorrow in her face, Sharif's heart twisted. She had lost the sister she loved. He felt an almost overwhelming urge to gather her in his arms and comfort her.

He must guard against such weakness. He must barricade his heart against any softness and concentrate on winning Holly's cooperation through logic.

"Believe me, this discovery of your sister's death is troubling," he said. "The police are certain to suspect me. It can only make my escape even more difficult."

The uncertainty vanished from Holly's eyes, to be replaced by sheer fury. Despite his good intentions, the sheikh saw, he had said precisely the wrong thing.

He didn't know what it was, but he figured she was about to tell him.

HER SISTER'S death troubled this man only because it made his escape more difficult? If Holly hadn't been so cold and muddy and so aware of their isolation, she'd have been tempted to slap his arrogant face.

"Don't you even care who killed her?" she cried. "She's the mother of your son. And if you or Zahad didn't kill her, maybe it was your enemies. Why did she have to die for your quarrel?"

Through the rolling patter of rain on the roof, she could hear his sharp intake of breath. "It was never my intention to bring harm to Jasmine," he said sadly. "And you are right. I do owe her a very large debt."

To her dismay, Holly found herself wanting to trust him. She struggled to hold on to her doubts. "I suppose Jazz could have gotten into trouble on her own. But to me, it's too big a coincidence. She disappears, and then you turn up and kidnap us."

"I know I can't convince you of my good character," the sheikh said. "But please, let's work together."

"What about tomorrow? Are we still going to the authorities?"

He stared past her, as if seeking some private source of wisdom. "Matters have changed. I need to examine the situation before I can choose a course of action."

"Because the police will suspect you?" she asked.

He nodded. "A murder charge will take much more time to disprove. It cannot simply be explained away like my behavior yesterday."

"All the more reason to turn yourself in, if you really are innocent!"

Sharif shook his head. "I will not relinquish my

son. Nor do I plan to become a sitting duck in your county jail. My enemies are not above hiring another prisoner to kill me.''

That stopped Holly cold. She'd seen for herself that someone was trying to assassinate the sheikh.

Yet she didn't have to stay here, unless Sharif forced her. She could go back, couldn't she?

But that would mean separating from Ben. Tears blurred her vision. She couldn't give him up, now more than ever.

As if on cue, the baby let out a series of hungry cries. Jazz was gone, but her child still needed Holly.

Maybe in time the sheikh would entrust her with the little boy while he resolved his legal problems. If he were imprisoned for a long time, he might even let her raise Ben.

Two pairs of dark eyes fixed on her, father and son. Both pleading.

Holly's resistance melted. A sense of calm fell over her, a momentary release from a grief too great to absorb all at once. Besides, she was too worn-out to make any major decisions tonight.

''Let me clean up,'' she said. ''Then I'll feed him.''

''Take my spare shirt from the closet,'' Sharif said. ''It's big enough to cover you, and it's dry.''

''Thanks.'' Dropping the bedspread, she carried the lightweight shirt into the bathroom off the alcove.

At least her escape attempt had demonstrated one thing, Holly reflected. Even when provoked, the sheikh didn't fly into a violent rage.

As she hung the garment over a hook, his haunting scent gave her a sense of his presence, as if he were here with her. She ached to lean against him, to let him absorb her fears and reassure her with his tenderness.

What was it about him that aroused such sensations? Holly, always the sensible one, had never understood how a woman could be swept away by passion.

She was beginning to get an inkling.

What would it be like to touch him? To smooth her palm across his rough cheek and feel his hard mouth claim hers?

She must be losing her mind! Even if the sheikh really was innocent of Jazz's death, he remained an enigma.

And what about Trevor? True, she didn't burn with desire for him, but the man loved her, and he deserved her loyalty.

Her thoughts in turmoil, Holly stripped off her stockings and the ruined wedding gown, and showered quickly. Above the tub, rain lashed against a rippled window.

After drying off, she slipped on the blue button-down shirt. The silky cloth fell tantalizingly to mid-thigh.

There was something seductive about the fabric. And a reassuring warmth, despite its delicate appearance.

She glanced into the full-length mirror on the back of the door, half-afraid to see how she looked after her experiences of the past dozen hours. There was a small cut on her neck from the shattered glass and a trace of darkness beneath her eyes, but the satiny shirt made her skin glow.

This was supposed to be her wedding night, she remembered. A night when she and Trevor merged, body and soul. How could she allow herself to imagine, even for an instant, how it would feel if Sharif smoothed the fabric over her breasts and lifted her onto the bed?

She emerged from the bathroom. ''Your turn.'' Then she saw that he had shed his robe and muddy shoes and sat cross-legged on the bed in sweatshirt and jeans, trying to feed Ben.

It was the first time the sheikh had appeared before her without a headdress or cap. His hair, which fell below the collar, was thick and ragged, as if he had been running his hands through it.

''Let me do that,'' she said, and he glanced up.

His casual attention intensified as he drank in the sight of her bare legs and clearly defined body. Fires lit inside his dark eyes.

''The baby!'' Holly said. ''You're dribbling formula on him.''

''Oh!'' His rueful smile carried an apology, and a hint of amusement. They both knew, after all, what had distracted him.

Briskly, she took the child and the bottle to a nearby chair. Putting distance between them helped focus her thoughts.

They returned immediately, agonizingly, to Jazz. And to Sharif's tacit admission that her death might have some connection with his enemies.

''Those men who shot at us,'' she said. ''Who are they and why do they hate you so much?''

Sharif rummaged through a linen closet and retrieved a blanket. ''Some years ago, I helped to free Alqedar from a dictator named Maimun Gozen. When we took back the palace in our capital city, I killed him in combat. Some of his supporters escaped and have vowed revenge."

"So they might have wanted to kill Ben, to punish you?" she asked. "And murdered Jazz when she wouldn't say where he was?"

"It is a possibility, and yet it does not entirely ring true." The sheikh wrapped the blanket around her. "There's a strong taboo among my people against cowardly attacks on women and children."

Warmth surrounded her, bringing relaxation and a sudden urge to yawn. "I suppose… I mean, she might have been carrying a lot of cash. People kill for that."

"I wish I could believe it were so simple a matter," Sharif said. "Then there would be no further threat to you or my son. As for myself, I am accustomed to taking precautions."

As she raised Ben to her shoulder to burp him, Holly's eyelids began to close. The sheikh took his son. "Lie down. I'll take over from here."

Holly didn't argue. Clutching the blanket, she stumbled toward the bed.

The next thing she knew, gray morning light woke her to the thrum of rain and the smell of coffee. Beside her, Ben slept in baby bliss.

Across the room, Sharif was buttering toast. Jeans hugged his slim hips, and the sweatshirt clung to his chest and shoulders. From this angle, she could see that his hair needed a good brushing. And, even more, a decent cut.

If only the morning could unfold at a lazy pace. If only they didn't have to…

Like a shock wave, reality rushed in. Jazz was dead. Never again would anyone see that lively face or hear that beautiful voice. The girl Holly had loved and protected since childhood had been robbed of her dreams.

She no longer felt in any immediate danger herself, however. At some point last night, without making a conscious decision, she had come to accept, at least tentatively, that Sharif might be innocent.

In the kitchenette, he had noticed her stirring. "Ah, you are awake. Good morning, Holly." His accent gave the greeting an invigorating lilt.

"Good morning." When she sat up, hugging her knees, the silken shirt surrounded her with an exotic aroma. "What's this made of? I've never worn material like this."

"That is synthetic Jubah cloth."

"Jubah cloth?" Holly remembered one of her clients raving about a dress she'd bought for a special occasion. "That's expensive, isn't it? But I didn't know it had been synthesized."

"It hadn't, until now." He poured a cup of coffee. "Cream and sugar?" He added them and came across the room with her mug.

The hot liquid proved strong and bitter, but she needed to jump-start her system. "I'm surprised you'd let me sleep in something so valuable."

"We're beginning to manufacture it in my home province of Bahrim," he said. "We hope that it will bring prosperity to my people."

"I hope so." Holly couldn't resist brushing her cheek against the soft collar.

"It looks lovely against your skin," Sharif said. "You are very fair." The words caressed her, raising a shimmer of unspoken longing.

"It's my Irish heritage," she said quickly. "It goes

with the red hair. But Jazz was the beauty of the family.''

''Not the only one,'' he murmured.

Holly knew she must be blushing, and searched for a more neutral subject. ''This synthetic Jubah…who actually owns the rights to it?''

''I do,'' he said. ''Along with Harry Haroun, the chemist who invented it,'' he said. ''His wife is my cousin Amy, which is short for Amineh. She has a business degree and is handling negotiations with distributors abroad.''

''Is she Zahad's sister?'' Holly asked. ''Or his cousin, too?''

''Neither. Her father was my father's younger brother. Zahad's mother was my mother's sister,'' he said.

''I hope there isn't going to be a quiz afterward,'' she sighed.

''I don't expect you to keep track of my family. Sometimes I can hardly keep track of them myself.'' He came to take her empty cup.

''I don't suppose you've changed your mind and decided to go the police after all?'' she asked.

''I am afraid not.''

''Sharif, I don't want to leave Ben,'' Holly said. ''But the more I think about it, well, it's not a good idea for me to stay here. Isn't there some way I can take him with me until things are resolved?''

The sheikh's fingers drummed against the table. ''If he really was the intended target, then allowing you to take him would put you in the eye of the hurricane,'' he said. ''In this case, I am afraid it is a bull's-eye.''

"And you consider him safer with you?" she demanded.

"For the moment. Unless, of course, I drop him while trying to change his diaper." He spared her a smile. "That is why, last night as you slept, I called my cousin Amy."

Her heart thudded. "The one who's going to help raise him, right?"

He nodded. "She's in Boston negotiating a contract for Jubah cloth. As soon as she can get here, I will arrange for her to take my son back to Alqedar. Then he will have a mother's care, and the protection of my palace guard."

A lump formed in Holly's throat. Ben, who'd awakened, lay beaming at her contentedly. So tiny and perfect, with large, intelligent eyes. Even after only a month, she knew his moods and his zesty spirit and his eager curiosity.

He was all that remained of her sister. And he had taken complete possession of her heart. How could she hand him to another woman?

"You are going to be married as soon as you return," Sharif reminded her, as if reading her thoughts. "You will have other children. But I will not."

"Why?"

Ignoring her question, he took out his cell phone. "I must call Zahad. We have arrangements to make."

"Sharif—" As she took a step toward him, the cold floor against her bare feet reminded Holly that she wasn't dressed. Besides, what could she say? She wasn't going to fly to the Middle East to play nursemaid, even if Sharif would allow it.

And he was right. Soon she would be married to Trevor, and this man would fade to a memory. As for

Ben, he had never really been hers, no matter how much her heart protested otherwise.

The sheikh dialed, listened, and then, frowning, folded away the device. "He does not answer."

"What does that mean?" Since Zahad had the car, they needed him to bring supplies. And to take them away from here when they were ready.

"His phone rings, but he doesn't answer. That is odd."

"Maybe he went out," she said. "Or he's in the shower."

"My cousin keeps the phone with him at all times." Standing to one side of the window, Sharif peered through the blinds. "If someone has taken him, our situation is grave indeed."

Holly bore no fondness for the scarred man who'd helped kidnap Ben. But without him, Sharif's chances of escaping his enemies would dwindle drastically. So would Ben's.

Despite her profoundly mixed feelings, she hoped Zahad would turn up. And soon.

# Chapter Five

It took Zahad only a minute to pry open the back door and turn off the security system at the Crestline View Clinic.

He'd been here three times before: first to check out the place before recommending it to Sharif, then to deliver a specimen essential to conception, and again two months ago in an attempt to locate the surrogate.

On the third visit, he'd deliberately arrived before the clinic opened and made a point of waiting for the clinic director near the back door. Surprised to find him there, she'd entered her password into the alarm system right in front of him. He was glad to find she hadn't changed it in the interim.

He hadn't been certain he would ever need the password, but it was a point of pride with Zahad to foresee and circumvent difficulties. His failure to notice the security camera yesterday still stung. One mistake had nearly ruined everything.

The rear entrance opened into a dim corridor smelling of antiseptic. His sneakers made no noise on the carpet as he passed the lab and a couple of examining rooms.

Medical facilities kept locked cabinets for their medications, but he didn't bother with those. If what he sought existed, it would be in Mrs. Wheaton's office.

An hour ago, Zahad had been busy laying in supplies at a twenty-four-hour store. He'd had no plans to come here until he heard on the radio that the dead woman in the desert had been identified as Hannah Jasmine Rivers.

It was now 6:37 a.m. Neither Mrs. Wheaton, her physician-partner, nor the rest of the staff was likely to arrive before eight-thirty, according to his previous observations. The clinic opened at nine.

The clinic director had begun avoiding Zahad's phone calls one month ago, which he now knew was when the baby had appeared at Holly Rivers's home. He needed to find the connection. If someone had threatened Mrs. Wheaton into silence, she might have written down some clue to the person's identity.

Zahad preferred to avoid contacting the woman directly. She might be under surveillance by either the police or the killer. Or she might be involved in a scheme herself.

Until he knew who posed a threat, he dared not proceed with arrangements for their return to Alqedar. Someone could be lying in wait, possibly someone they trusted.

Even in the dim morning light, he had no trouble reading Mrs. Wheaton's name on an office door. His tools, readily manipulated through his surgical gloves, made short work of the lock.

Inside, Zahad flicked on his flashlight. The office was of modest size and sparsely furnished with a pine desk and a matching file cabinet.

The framed certificates on the walls were too small to hide a safe, and, besides, he doubted Mrs. Wheaton would have gone to great lengths to hide a note. His hope was that, like many professionals, she had the habit of jotting down the names of her callers and the nature of their business.

The desk wasn't locked. The first two drawers, he discovered when he prowled through them, contained stationery supplies, invoices, receipts and lists of government regulations.

In the third drawer lay a messy stack of used memo pads. Glancing at them, Zahad saw that Noreen doodled as she spoke. Most of the small pages were decorated with images of women's faces.

Despite his urgency, handling the papers through surgical gloves slowed him. Also, although he read English well, it took a while to adjust to scanning messy handwritten notes by flashlight.

At last a phrase caught his eye. "Jazz knows." The handwriting slanted so unevenly that he had to squint to decipher the rest. "Stall them."

What was it that Jasmine had discovered? Whom had Mrs. Wheaton been instructed to stall? Zahad had a strong suspicion he knew the answer to the last question, but he tucked the note into his windbreaker pocket and continued reading through the stack. He needed more. Who had called Noreen? What was so important that Jasmine had been murdered over it?

Outside, a car rumbled into the driveway. Headlights raked the window.

By the digital clock on the desk, it was 6:58. Could someone be coming on duty already?

Adrenaline began to pump as the vehicle halted and the engine died. Two doors slammed.

Through the blinds, he peered into the light rain. Although the people were out of sight, Zahad made out the blue and white markings of a Harbor View police car.

He shoved the drawer shut and scooted from the office. Which entrance would the newcomers use? Most likely the back, the same way he'd come, but if he guessed wrong he would run right into them.

Inside his pocket, his phone pulsed. He couldn't pause to answer it. In the corridor, he braced himself, listening intently.

From outside the back door, a woman's voice said, "Her car isn't in its reserved space, officer. I can't imagine what's happened. You saw the mess at her condo."

"You're certain Mrs. Wheaton didn't live with anyone?" a man's voice enquired.

"Yes." Keys jingled.

"Was it like her to bring someone home to spend the night?"

"No. Besides, I always pick her up for breakfast on Tuesdays. They have a pancake special at the coffee shop down the street." A key scraped. "Gee, the door's open. I wonder—"

Zahad made a dash for the front. There was no point in trying to sneak out. At this point, any policeman worth his salt would suspect there'd been a break-in.

When he pushed the safety bar and went out, he half expected to run into reinforcements, but the sidewalk was empty. It took all his self-control to close the door quietly, strip off his gloves and toss them into the nearest trash dumpster.

Crestline Avenue's four lanes carried sparse traffic

at this hour. As he sauntered across the street, Zahad shrugged deep into his windbreaker, hunkering down against the weather and hiding his face.

Diagonally opposite stood a convenience store that sold coffee and doughnuts. Zahad had parked behind it in an alley, hoping that at this early hour no one would notice his pickup truck with its camper shell.

Ducking into the store, he skirted the front mat to avoid setting off a bell and pretended to study a rack of magazines near the front window. The clerk was busy pouring coffee for a man in blue overalls. Another man sat eating a doughnut at a small table, facing away from Zahad.

Another police car came down the street, its siren wailing as it turned into the clinic parking lot. The police had gone onto full alert.

No wonder. Their placid town had just suffered a double kidnapping, the death of a missing resident, and now...

Judging by what he'd overheard, Noreen Wheaton's condo had been ransacked and she was unaccounted for. Had she staged her own disappearance? Or been abducted, perhaps killed?

Zahad could see no obvious connection to Sharif's enemies. Yet, because the sheikh's son had been conceived at the clinic, he couldn't discount such a possibility.

He was no closer to knowing the truth than he had been an hour ago. And there were three policemen fanning out from the front of the clinic. One of them started toward the convenience store. Through the glass, his gaze met Zahad's.

"YOU DON'T need to tell me what's happened! It's made the TV even here in Boston. Both your faces were on the evening news, stealing a bride and a baby! Aren't you ashamed?''

The sharp edge of Amy Haroun's tongue could be felt across the continent. Sharif wondered why he hadn't noticed before how much his cousin, when angry, sounded like their Aunt Selima chewing out a dishonest fishmonger.

"Amy, I need you," he said into his phone, hoping to cut off the tirade.

"You don't need me! You need a lawyer!"

"Listen." Switching from English to Baharalik, he told her about the discovery of Jazz's body. As he talked, he kept watching the clearing outside the cabin for Zahad.

It was past 8:30 a.m. Several more calls to his aide had gone unanswered.

Holly had given the baby a bath and changed him into warm pajamas. Now she sat before the fire, crooning to the infant.

Auburn hair framed her heart-shaped face as she sang a lullaby. Ben cooed and waved his hands as if trying to sing along.

It was obvious that she and the child loved each other. Sharif hated to hurt her by taking his son away, but he needed to get Ben to safety.

First, however, he needed to make sure where safety lay. With Amy, he hoped.

"So, Zahad has pulled a disappearing act and you are stuck in the woods with another man's wife-to-be," grumbled his cousin. "And you want me to come there and rescue you?"

"Not rescue me. Just the baby," he said. "I will take care of myself."

"As if you have done such a wonderful job so far!" she said.

From her agitated tone, he could imagine Amy plucking out one of her jewelled combs and skimming back her dark hair. It was a nervous habit so ingrained that she sometimes absentmindedly tried it while wearing a headscarf.

"But you will come," he said quietly. "You are one of the few people on this earth I trust completely."

"Here is what I will do." Even in Baharalik, her voice revealed a hint of an English accent. Like Zahad, Amy had studied in Britain rather than America; it was in London that she'd met her husband, Harry. "I will fly to Los Angeles and secure an attorney for you. Then I will take the baby."

"Thank you," he said.

"Do let me know when our mutual friend turns up, will you?" she added. "Perhaps he has gone to kidnap a bride of his own."

"I don't think so." Sharif couldn't help but smile at the idea of his no-nonsense aide waxing romantic. "I look forward to seeing you, Amy."

After she rang off, he tried Zahad's number again. This time, it clicked after three rings as if someone had answered.

"Zahad?" he said. "Is it you?"

A burst of static, and then nothing.

Sharif's heart rate accelerated. What did such a response mean, after his calls had gone unanswered all morning?

Mobile phones could be unreliable. Ordinarily, he would have called Zahad right back.

It was possible, however, that the phone had fallen

into the wrong hands. Because the recipient might have accidentally disconnected while trying to trace the call, he couldn't risk redialing.

"We need to leave," he told Holly. "Quickly. Something may have happened to Zahad. It would not be like him to reveal where we are, but we must take no chances."

To her credit, she didn't ask a lot of questions, only "Where can we go without a car?"

He'd forgotten that handicap. Why had he ever allowed Zahad to leave him here without transport? In retrospect, the sheikh could see that he'd been too preoccupied with his son to weigh all the possibilities.

"The rain's easing," he noted, and immediately reproached himself for sounding like an idiot. They were miles from the nearest shops, and even if they managed to walk that far, then what? The two of them, muddy and carrying a baby, would be about as conspicuous on foot in this region as they would be riding camels. "A cab? No, I fear not. They will be the first ones notified to watch for us."

"I could ask a friend to pick us up," Holly said.

Of course; it was the obvious solution. Perhaps too obvious. Was she trying to trick him? A few hours ago, she'd done her best to flee.

Sharif stared across the cabin into her honest brown eyes. Against his best intentions, he'd developed a sense of closeness with this woman.

Besides, under the circumstances, he had to trust her. Not only did she offer their only chance of escape, but eventually he would need Holly's testimony to clear him of kidnapping.

He handed her the phone and carried the baby to the bed. "Who will you call?" he asked.

THE FIRST PERSON who came to mind was Trevor. Since her teen years, it was on him that Holly had relied for advice and support.

But the police would be tapping his phone. Plus, she could hardly ask her fiancé to help her protect Sharif after he'd made a shambles of their wedding.

Oddly, she felt only mild embarrassment about the chaos she'd left behind at the church. Shouldn't she be heartbroken at the interruption of her plans and anxious to return for her wedding night?

Instead, this cabin had become her refuge, a place where she'd discovered sensual feelings that were new to her. A place where she, Sharif and Ben seemed almost like a family.

In any case, she couldn't call Trevor. If nothing else, as a lawyer he was an officer of the court. With no attorney-client privilege involved, he would have to notify the authorities.

"Alice," she said aloud.

"Who?" the sheikh asked as he resumed his post by the window.

"My boss at the salon," she explained. "She was my matron of honor."

"The older lady at the church?" he said. "Are you certain she would help you?"

"She loves Ben like a grandmother," Holly said. "She'd do anything to keep him safe. So would I."

She tried not to think about what that safety would require. Never seeing her nephew again. Leaving his upbringing to a woman she'd never met, the one Sharif had been talking to in that strange language.

The man's jaw worked. "The police are likely monitoring her phone. Is there some way to reach her that they might not anticipate?"

Holly visualized the salon, twenty minutes before opening time. Alice would be there along with most of the staff, setting up their stations and drinking coffee.

"Marta has a cell phone," she said. "She's the other manicurist. If I can just remember her number!"

She'd needed it whenever Jazz took off unexpectedly for a gig, to arrange for Marta to cover the extra hours. Not even the indulgent Alice could be expected to tolerate a manicurist standing up clients, and Holly hadn't wanted her sister to lose her job.

The number came back to her, and she dialed. She waited tensely through a couple of rings until Marta answered.

"I need to talk to Alice," she said without preamble.

"Holly? Is that you?" The manicurist's voice rose an octave.

"Yes. Don't say anything to anyone! Is she there?"

"You bet!" Away from the phone, a few excited words were exchanged, and then Alice came on the line.

"Is this who I think it is?" she demanded. "Are you all right? How's Ben?"

"He's fine. Listen—"

"Where are you?"

"Alice, please listen!" Holly said.

Her employer was too overwrought to comply. "Did you hear about Jazz? It's so horrible."

"Yes, I did," she said.

"That sheikh, has he hurt you? Did you get away?"

"Things aren't what they seem." Holly could see that Alice would never cooperate unless she understood the basic situation, so she didn't beat around the bush. "The sheikh is Ben's father."

"What?" A shocked silence fell.

"Whoever killed Jazz may also be trying to kill us," she went on. "Someone shot at our car yesterday. I can't explain the whole thing, but we need your help."

"Does Trevor know what's going on?" Alice interjected. "What about the police?"

"No, they don't, and they mustn't find out yet." Holly could see this wasn't going to be as easy as she'd hoped. "We have to stay in hiding."

From the window, the sheikh signaled her urgently. "Hang up! Someone's here!"

"We've got an emergency. I'll call you back," Holly said. "Don't you or Marta talk to anybody until you hear from me! This is life or death, Alice."

In the ensuing pause, she sensed that her friend was wavering. Finally Alice said, "If I don't hear from you in half an hour, I'm calling the cops!"

"Hurry!" said Sharif.

"I'll call you as soon as I can." She pressed End and, obeying the sheikh's gestures, flattened herself against the wall. "Who is it?"

"A pickup truck." Then, with relief, "It's Zahad." He observed for a moment longer. "I don't see anyone following him. Just in case, take the baby into the bathroom."

Although his advice made sense, Holly's nerves wouldn't take much more. "I'm not cowering and hiding! If it's safe enough for you, it's safe enough for me."

When she'd told Alice not to call the police, she realized, it meant she'd accepted the argument that the authorities couldn't guarantee her safety, or Ben's. She'd thrown in her lot with the sheikh, and she intended to be his equal partner, not a tagalong.

"Keep the baby back," he muttered.

Through the window, she watched the dark-haired man approach along the edge of the woods, stopping several times to observe the cabin and the surroundings through the mist. Now that he'd shaved his beard and mustache, Holly wasn't sure she would have recognized him.

Sharif rapped several times on the window in an apparent code, then went to the door. When his cousin came inside, he stared at Holly in surprise. "Why did you untie her?"

"I needed her help with the baby." The sheikh spoke abruptly, as if unwilling to reveal that they had formed the beginnings of a friendship. If, indeed, they had.

"Were you also forced to remove her clothing?" Zahad asked, scrutinizing Holly.

She shrank inside the oversize shirt. Until now, her bare legs hadn't bothered her, but the newcomer's presence made her uncomfortable. "My gown got dirty." Not wanting to explain that she'd tried to flee through the mud, she added, "It isn't easy caring for a baby, you know!"

"So the women of the palace tell me." She could have sworn a smile tugged at the corners of Zahad's mouth, but he quickly resumed his customary stern expression. "It is a good thing I anticipated that you would need new garments."

"Why did you not answer your phone?" Sharif asked.

"It was too dangerous." From a shoulder bag, the

aide began unloading baby supplies, food, hair dye and some folded clothing. "I went to the clinic. Noreen Wheaton has disappeared and the police are looking for her."

"Disappeared?" Holly said.

The man nodded. "Her condo was ransacked. Also, at the clinic, I found this."

He handed a note to Sharif, who read it aloud. "'Jazz knows. Stall them.' What is this?"

"I found no name and no explanation, but it would appear that someone called and informed Mrs. Wheaton of a change in their circumstances," Zahad said. "My guess is that it happened when the baby turned up."

"This is not likely to be the work of Maimun's followers," Sharif observed.

"No, but it has complicated our situation." The aide grimaced. "Heaven knows what else has transpired that we may also be suspected of. One could hardly imagine that claiming one baby would become so complicated!"

"I'm surprised you could get in and out of the clinic without being caught," she said.

"That is why Zahad is my security chief," Sharif said. "The man never ceases to amaze me."

Zahad ducked his head, as if embarrassed by the praise. "At a store nearby, a policeman questioned me, but only as a possible witness," he said. "By good luck, another customer mistook me for someone he had seen come into the shop ten minutes earlier. As a result, I was able to leave before anyone connected me to the abductor who is all over TV."

He went back to the truck and returned with more

supplies, along with a couple of guns. Sharif regarded them with distaste, but did not object.

"Also I bought a motorcycle for myself," Zahad said. "It's in the truck, which I will leave with you, Sharif. Not that either of us will be going very far today."

"You think it's too dangerous to try to leave the country?" the sheikh asked.

"Indeed, yes. Perilous both to cross the border, and to return home," he said. "Until we find out what's going on, we might never make it as far as the palace. We cannot discount the possibility that Noreen decided to double-cross us by selling out to our enemies. Or that there is a conspiracy against you that reaches to high places in Alqedar."

Holly shuddered. How had her sister gotten involved with such dangerous people?

"Amy is coming as soon as she can catch a flight," the sheikh said. "Once Ben is gone, I can take greater risks."

"What makes you so sure these people won't shoot at Amy, too?" Holly blurted. "It seems to me you're ignoring your best resource, which is me. I knew my sister as well as anyone. Maybe I can help you find out what happened, who she might have confided in, that kind of thing."

"You did not even know she was a surrogate," Sharif pointed out.

"Well, I know who her friends are! Some of them, anyway." Holly was already beginning to regret her bravado as Zahad frowned at her. "There's Griff, for instance. He's the one who brought Ben to me."

"The police have no doubt already questioned him," the aide said.

"If they can find him." Holly hadn't been close to the scruffy musician, but she'd known him for a long time. "He has a drug conviction and he claims the police set him up. He doesn't trust them."

"And you think you could find this man?" Sharif asked.

"I have to call Alice back anyway," Holly said. "She might have Griff's pager number. Jazz gave it to her so she could hire his band to play at a party last Fourth of July."

"Very well," Sharif said. "It is worth a try, considering that we have no other leads at the moment."

"Amateurs have a great talent for screwing things up," said Zahad.

"Do you think Griff would talk to you?" she shot back. "I doubt it!"

"This woman is strong-willed," he told Sharif. "She reminds me of Amy." To Holly, he said, "That is not a compliment."

She turned to the sheikh. "I like your cousin already." Seeing his puzzled expression, she added, "I mean Amy, of course."

Zahad laughed. "When a woman seizes upon a course of action, you might as well stand in the path of an armored tank. Well, I have brought some cloned phones to reduce the chance of our being traced. Use one of them, and be brief."

Holly took the one he handed her. It went against her ethics to use a stolen cell phone number, but she didn't see that she had much choice.

"I will go unload the motorcycle." Zahad started out.

"I'll help." Sharif moved to join him.

"You plan to leave her in here with the phone? Heaven knows who she will call!"

"I have faith in her." The other man began to protest in the alien language, but Sharif stood his ground. At last the two went out together.

Holly stared at the phone. Zahad was right. She could call Alice, as she'd promised, and help Sharif contact Griff. Or she could call the police.

It boiled down to a question of whom she trusted most.

## Chapter Six

An image burned inside Holly's mind. It was her sister's body on TV, the tattooed arm highlighted by the blare of lights.

She'd searched for Jazz for a month. She'd filed police reports, and talked to an investigator who'd promised to make inquiries. But they hadn't found her sister until it was too late.

No matter how diligent they might be, the officers were only human. If they arrested the sheikh, they would concentrate their immediate efforts on grilling him.

Meanwhile, the killer would escape. Or, perhaps, strike again.

Holly wasn't sure the men from Alqedar could accomplish any more than the police. But something about Sharif filled her with a confidence that defied explanation.

She checked her watch. Twenty-two minutes had passed. It was time to call Alice.

The salon owner answered Marta's phone on the first ring. "This better be you!"

"Of course it's me. You're not going to rat on us, right? You promised!"

"Don't worry. Marta and I swore everyone to se-crecy," her boss replied. "I hope I'm not making a terrible mistake. Now what's this about the sheikh being Ben's father, Holly?"

She took a deep breath and plunged in. "Jazz was a surrogate mother. He hired her through the Crestline View Clinic."

"Jazz? No way! He's making this up."

"He showed me his contract with the clinic," she said. "And the baby—their eyes are exactly alike."

A warning note crept into Alice's voice. "I saw a TV show where a kidnap victim got attached to her captor. It's some kind of mental trick they use. Don't forget that he grabbed you and forced you into the car."

"No, he didn't," Holly said. "He took the baby and I jumped in after him. Then someone shot at us. This case is a lot bigger than the police realize, and they're wasting their time focusing on Sharif. Alice, I need Griff's pager number."

"You're not planning to investigate this yourself!"

"We have to," Holly said. "Please, Alice."

Her friend sighed. "I gave it to the cops already. They questioned me, of course, and I'm sure they've talked to him by now, too."

"If they can reach him. You know how leery he is," Holly pointed out. "Come on, what can it hurt to give me the number?"

"Okay, but listen." Alice was, as usual, thinking on her feet. "Why don't you meet me somewhere? Give me the baby. I'll take care of him while you're…doing whatever crazy thing you've decided to do."

It was a kind offer, but impossible. "That might

put you in danger. Besides, Sharif won't part with his son." She decided not to mention that Ben was going to be handed over to a cousin. "I'm sorry, Alice."

There was a long pause. Then, "Well, all right. Here's Griff's number." She read it off. "And Holly?"

"Yes?"

"I won't volunteer anything about this conversation, but if the police ask me a direct question, I won't lie, either."

"I understand," she said. "You're already doing more than anyone could reasonably expect."

"Take care of yourself," Alice said. "And let me know when you need me to take care of that sweet little baby. Anytime!"

"I will. And thanks." Holly clicked off.

Through the window, she saw Sharif and Zahad talking next to the truck. A glimmer of sunlight had broken through the clouds, making water droplets glisten like crystal ornaments on the dark trees.

She couldn't page Griff until she conferred with the sheikh. For one thing, she didn't know what return phone number to leave.

Inside the cabin, all was deceptively quiet. Ben slept, curled on the bed like a kitten. On TV, the weather report showed another storm would be moving in later that day, bringing high winds and rain.

At least now they had the pickup truck, so they weren't stuck. Still, the prospect of a storm made her edgy.

Outside, Zahad kicked his motorbike into action and sped away. Sharif headed for the cabin.

The sheikh moved with tensed readiness, like a

fighter. The insistent maleness of the man infused every movement.

He'd mentioned that he was a widower. What kind of life did he lead at home? Was there a woman who had earned the right to strip off that sweatshirt and hold him through the night?

She pictured a bed hung with a canopy. The woman would have long dark hair and mysterious eyes, and yet she would feel just as Holly did, eager and hungry and a little awed by this man...

"We have several new developments in the case of Harbor View's kidnapped bride." The TV announcer's voice snapped her back to reality, and she hurried to turn up the volume.

"As reported earlier, Hannah Jasmine Rivers, the woman whose body was found in the desert last night, was the mother of the baby boy who vanished with his aunt just before her wedding yesterday."

The anchorman, a fortyish fellow with perfect hair, stared straight into the camera as if about to unburden his heart's deepest secret.

"Hannah Rivers apparently served as a surrogate mother for the Crestline View Clinic in Harbor View. According to an employee of the clinic, the father of that baby is the alleged kidnapper, Sheikh Sharif Al-Khalil."

Sharif, who had slipped into the room, stood watching with reluctant respect. "These news people are good at their job, which is gossip. My aunt Selima would approve."

"Police have declined to confirm the report or to speculate on what it might mean," the man went on. "However, they did confirm that the director of the surrogacy clinic, Noreen Wheaton, vanished this morning. Her home and office had been rifled.''

So many interwoven threads, Holly thought. But what was the overall pattern?

The announcer had his own theory, he revealed with his next comment. ''Is this an old-fashioned crime of revenge?'' he intoned. ''Was Hannah Jasmine Rivers killed because she refused to surrender her son? Is Noreen Wheaton in danger because she failed to enforce the surrogacy agreement?

''Fears mount for the safety of the baby's aunt, Holly Jeannette Rivers, the missing bride. We'll bring you updates as soon as they come in.''

Holly muted the sound. ''They're ready to try, convict and sentence you!''

''I wonder who told them about Ben's paternity. The clinic's records are supposed to be secret.''

''An employee?'' Holly said. ''What about that man who witnessed the contract—Manuel Estrellas?''

''Whatever's going on, he probably knows more about it than we do,'' Sharif agreed. ''First, however, we need to find the last man to see your sister alive. Did you get his number?''

''Yes,'' she said. ''Do you want me to page him?''

''I'll do it.'' Taking the phone, Sharif dialed the number she'd written, tapped in another one and hung up. ''We can't receive calls on a cloned phone, so we have to give him my number.''

Ben awoke with a lusty wail. Before she could react, Sharif tucked the phone away and collected the boy onto his lap. ''Would you prepare a bottle for me?''

''Sure.'' If only Alice could see the melting look in the man's eyes as he played with the child, she wouldn't doubt their intimate connection. "Where did Zahad go?"

"He likes to keep moving," the sheikh said vaguely. She could see there was no point in inquiring further.

When father and son were settled, Holly went to check the items that the aide had brought. A pair of jeans and a V-necked sweater looked like the right size, although the tennis shoes were a bit large. "Are these for me? I'm amazed—they might actually fit."

"My cousin has rough edges, but he observes everything. Very accurately, too." Sharif turned his attention to his son. He smiled down at the baby, who had laid one tiny hand on his wrist while eating. The tenderness they both felt for this baby had brought them together, Holly reflected in a burst of warmth.

"I guess I should change, then." Holding the clothes, she started toward the bathroom.

"Take the phone with you, in case Griff calls. If he hears a man answer, he might hang up."

"Where is it?" Holly asked.

Sharif's chin jerked downward. "In my pocket. Sorry, I have no free hands."

The teasing gaze he slanted at Holly made her aware of how intimately her silky shirt draped over the roundness of her breasts. No doubt he could see how the nipples tightened in the cool air.

Slowly, she laid her fresh clothes aside. To retrieve the phone, she would have to reach into the front of Sharif's sweatshirt. The prospect of touching his chest stirred a hot, restless ache, and she took a step backward. "I—maybe we should wait till you're done feeding Ben."

"Do I make you nervous?" One eyebrow lifted. "I

apologize if I appear to be such a savage. I promise that I will not attack you.''

''Don't be ridiculous!'' She could hardly explain that the problem was her, not him. She was so keenly aware of Sharif that her entire body seemed to vibrate. ''I just don't want to disturb the baby.''

''He's fine.'' She could have sworn the sheikh purposely assumed an expression of bland innocence. ''Go right ahead.''

He was daring her, and she didn't intend to back off.

She reached past his arm and the baby. The aura of the man surrounded her, and she paused. How could his subtle male scent make her so intensely aware of her own femininity?

''Something wrong?'' Sharif asked.

''Not a thing,'' said Holly.

When she slid her hand into his front pocket, her palm grazed the wall of his chest. Through the knit fabric, she felt the tautness of his muscles. His eyelids lowered, giving him the hooded aspect of a hawk.

''Where's the phone?''

''Wrong pocket,'' he said.

''You could have told me!'' She yanked out her hand.

''That would have spoiled your fun.'' The corners of his mouth lifted.

''Cheeky, aren't you?''

''I hope you're not giving up so easily.''

''Not at all.'' She reached into the facing pocket, and her fingers closed over the phone.

Their faces were only inches apart. His mouth was so strong, so close. So ready.

With one arm, he caught Holly against him, poised

off-balance above the baby. "Hey!" she protested. "I thought you had no free hand!"

"I lied," he murmured. "Do you object?"

She knew she ought to say yes. Or no. The funny thing was, she couldn't remember which answer meant what. So she might as well find out what he would do next.

"Well, as long as we're here..." He didn't finish his thought and she relaxed, just for an instant. But it was long enough for him to guide her mouth down to his.

The contact felt shockingly intimate. She shouldn't be kissing this stranger, this fierce man of the desert. Yet hot passion invaded her veins, melting her will to resist.

His tongue probed inside her lips, lightly but firmly. A shudder ran through Holly. He was taking more of her than she'd intended to give, yet she couldn't pull away.

Sharif's hand feathered across her neck and ran down her back, smoothing the soft shirt. The restrained power in his touch fascinated her. She wanted to bury her hands in his hair and urge him on.

The force of her desire threatened everything that Holly knew about herself. Everything that was safe and familiar. To make supreme pleasure shine in his eyes, she would give...

A face intruded into her thoughts. A face she knew so well, gazing at her with rueful admiration.

Trevor.

Shame rushed through her. How could she be acting this way? How could she treat the man she'd promised to marry so badly? Awkwardly, Holly pulled away.

"No." The sheikh tightened his one-armed grip. In his lap, Ben cooed winningly, inviting her to stay close.

Like father, like son, she thought.

"I can't do this," she said. "I'm engaged to marry Trevor."

With a sharp exhalation, Sharif released her. "I apologize. You belong to another man. I have no right to intrude."

"It's my fault as much as yours," she said miserably.

His gaze grew opaque. "Go and get dressed."

She straightened and picked up the clothes, then remembered that she needed shampoo. When she checked the objects on the table, she saw that Zahad had left several boxes of hair dye, along with a pair of scissors. "I guess I should use some of this. In case we decide to go out."

The sheikh nodded. "Perhaps when you are finished, you can do something to change my appearance, as well. Considering your profession, you should have no difficulty."

"This place doesn't exactly come with the latest equipment," she said, "but I can manage."

It was a relief to focus on a specific task. After examining the colors available, Holly picked out a package of dark rinse and went into the bathroom.

EXCITEMENT SURGED through Sharif's body. His need for Holly sang in his blood, into the most hidden reaches of his mind. Never had he experienced such delicious torment.

The woman had returned his passion with an equal measure of her own. For a brief moment, the sheikh had allowed himself to long for things he could not have. For her red hair spilling across his pillow, her lips curving in invitation, her arms reaching for him. This woman in his bed, by his side.

He must accept the truth. Holly could not be his. She belonged to another man and another world.

Even if she were free, how could he keep her? He was not a domesticated man that a woman could depend on. At a young age, violence had been drilled into his reflexes. War had become his natural state.

He would not make Holly dependent, only to let her down. Only to lose her, as he had lost Yona.

He had held joy once, like a fragile ceramic vessel. Without meaning to, he had crushed it to shards. The sharp pieces cut him still.

Nine years ago, his wife could have gone to Europe for medical care, but she had clung to him, determined to bear their child in their homeland. And he, selfishly, had agreed.

After the liberation of their home province, Sharif might have stayed with her. He could have sent Zahad in his stead, to fight in their country's capital. But having tasted victory in Bahrim, he had thirsted for more, and left his cousin in charge of the palace's defenses.

The sheikh had not even been present when his wife died. Unable to gaze into her face, to speak his love, to hold her hands. He had been too busy fighting.

It haunted him still, this terrible absence. That she must have cried out for him, and received only silence. He had betrayed her love.

In Sharif's arms, Ben wriggled. Realizing that the

boy probably needed to be changed, Sharif took him to the small table by the fire.

The process came more easily this time. His son had a cooperative nature. Perhaps that was a good thing. In the future, he hoped that Alqedar would need diplomats more than warriors.

On television, the weatherman was predicting a major storm, the biggest of the season. It seemed as if the elements were determined to isolate them.

He lifted the baby against his shoulder. The little head came up, and two shiny eyes peered into his.

Love flooded through Sharif, so powerful that the breath caught in his throat. He might armor himself against his yearning for a wife, but he could not deny the power that this child held over him.

He had thought he could produce a son and then simply entrust him to Amy and Aunt Selima. The child had been intended as a gift to Bahrim.

From the first time he saw the ultrasound picture of his son, however, Sharif's heart had been taken captive. Now he must protect the child at any cost.

The bathroom door opened. Even had he not heard it, he felt a change in the atmosphere when Holly returned. The fragrance of her skin and the brightness of her spirit filled the room.

She tossed her borrowed shirt onto the bed. "I can wash that by hand, if you've got some mild detergent."

"We have more important matters to..." He stopped, on catching sight of her changed appearance.

Gone was the sweep of auburn, replaced by a dark brown pageboy. She hadn't altered the length except to cut bangs that fell across her forehead.

The new style altered the proportions of her face,

making her cheeks appear wider and her mouth fuller. Against the stark coloring, her light skin gave her an air of sensuous fragility.

"Well?" she said. "Is it that bad?"

Bad enough that he wanted to resume where they had left off, with a kiss that deepened into something that no man should contemplate with another man's bride. "You will not be easily recognized," he said in as level a tone as he could summon. "Can you transform me as well?"

Stopping by the table, Holly fingered another of the boxes that Zahad had left. "Your cousin has good sense. He didn't expect me to turn you into a blond surfer."

"That would hardly be possible." He hoped she did not hear the gruff note in his voice. "What color shall I be?"

"Medium brown," Holly said, placing a chair by the sink. "You need a trim, too. Who cuts your hair at home?"

"The palace barber." After settling Ben in a large wicker basket near the hearth, Sharif sat down.

"You're sure it isn't the palace butcher?"

He chuckled. "Is it that bad? You cannot blame him. He has to catch me on the run."

He had taken some small pride in not becoming a decadent male who satisfied his vanity with fancy haircuts and scented shaving lotions. Now he wondered if he hadn't been foolish to think a decent haircut would offend his masculinity.

"This could be messy. I need to cover you with something." In a drawer, Holly found a vinyl tablecloth, which she draped over his shoulders. "Let's see

if we can't lift and lighten you into complete ano-
nymity.''

The sheikh was not eager to be either lifted or light-
ened. However, he leaned back over the sink and
yielded to Holly's ministrations.

She worked with steady efficiency as she sham-
pooed and rinsed him, then combed and snipped his
thick hair. Her touch on his scalp and the light pull
of the scissors had a lulling impact.

As soon as she finished cutting, Holly applied the
coloring agent. The sharp smell of chemicals filled
the air.

Attentively, she wiped drips from his forehead.
''We'll have to let that sit for a while.''

''It didn't take you long to change your hair
color,'' he pointed out.

''It's easier to go darker,'' she said. ''You know,
you've got great hair.''

''Excuse me?''

''It's thick and has wonderful texture. Just coarse
enough to style easily.'' As she talked, Holly
scrubbed residue from the sink and counter. ''You're
lucky to have a hint of natural curl, too.''

''It helps defeat my enemies.'' The sheikh spoke
as solemnly as he could. ''They become fascinated
by my texture and curl, and while they're staring at
it, I kill them.''

A peal of laughter split the air. ''You've got a sense
of humor!''

''You doubted it?'' He feigned a hurt expression.

''Never!'' Amusement softened her features and
made her eyes sparkle. At this moment, Sharif could
not imagine how he would return to Alqedar without
her.

Then abruptly, she blurted, "Oh, dear!" He followed Holly's line of sight to discover what had dismayed her. It was, as usual, the TV. He was beginning to hate the thing.

Right now, Trevor Samuelson's face filled the screen. The man was reclaiming his fiancée, even from a distance. A rival, Sharif reflected, who could not and should not be beaten.

Holly turned up the sound. "...and I'm asking this man to release my wife-to-be. She's no threat to you. Just please let her go."

"We understand that you're offering a reward?" Pulling back, the camera showed a woman reporter standing beside him in front of a sprawling, Mediterranean-style house.

"I'll pay ten thousand dollars for information leading to her safe return." Trevor's face looked pouchy. Sleepless from a short-circuited wedding night, no doubt. "Someone must have seen them. Someone has to know something. I'll make it worth their while."

"Here's the number of the police department." It flashed on the screen, followed by another. "And here's one for Mr. Samuelson's office, if any of our viewers would rather speak with you directly."

Holly hugged herself. "Sharif," she said. "I ought to call him."

He was trying to marshall his arguments when his own phone rang. Holly flinched, then, at his nod, she answered it. "Yes?... Griff, it's me! Holly!"

They had reached their target. Sharif only hoped the man could help them.

And that if he were the killer, they wouldn't walk blindly into his grasp.

# *Chapter Seven*

It took Holly a minute to reassure Griff that she wasn't being held against her will. He made her explain the circumstances of her abduction in detail.

"Let's meet somewhere," he said when she finished. "I want to see for myself that you're all right."

"Have you talked to the police?" she asked.

"No way." His hoarseness reminded her that, although it was midmorning, musicians kept late hours. "They paged me but when I realized it was the cops, I got off the line quick."

"You're hiding?"

"Damn straight," said the drummer. "If the police decide your sheikh didn't kill Jazz, they'll come after me next. I'm not letting them frame me again."

"Where are you?" she asked.

"A pay phone. I'm not calling from anywhere they could trace."

"Griff," she said. "Do you have any idea who killed my sister?"

"I wish I did!"

"Why did she run away before Ben was born?" she asked. "Why did she send him to me? You're the only person who knows what she was thinking."

In the background over the phone, she could hear traffic noises. "I've already been at this spot too long," Griff said. "Let's meet."

He named the Mexican restaurant where Alice's Independence Day party had been held. Located in the town of Placentia, about ten miles from Harbor View, it offered some secluded booths where they could talk.

"I—I guess so." To Sharif, Holly whispered, "He wants to meet." The sheikh nodded.

"Come alone," Griff said.

"I can't." Hoping he wouldn't hang up, she quickly added, "I may be in danger, and Ben, too. We need Sharif to protect us."

"Protect you? You're sure about that?"

"He's a good man," she told the musician. "He's in the same boat you are, when it comes to the police. So we're trying to find some leads they might miss."

"And he needs you to help him?" Griff grumbled. "Well, that's your choice, I guess. Okay, he can come on one condition."

"What's that?"

"You bring the baby, too," he said. "I miss the little guy."

"Sure." They had no one to leave Ben with, anyway.

"See ya in an hour." Without waiting for her goodbye, the musician clicked off.

Sharif raised an eyebrow questioningly. Holly explained about the meeting place.

"He didn't act odd in any way?" the sheikh asked. "Nothing to indicate this might be a trap?"

"He seemed normal, although I'm not sure I'd know if he *was* planning something." She'd been surprised at how protective Griff acted, but that was hardly suspicious.

"Very well, we'll go. I will advise Zahad." He dialed the phone. "Busy."

"Who do you suppose he's talking to?" she mused.

"He's on the Internet," Sharif said. "Digging up rumors and hopefully a few kernels of truth from our country. Well, if you can't beat them, join them, isn't that how the saying goes? I will send him an e-mail."

Opening his laptop, he attached the phone to the modem. As he typed, Holly peered outside. Storm clouds gathering across the sun gave the landscape a sepia tinge, and branches shivered in gusts of wind. She hoped the rain would hold off until after their rendezvous.

After Sharif finished, she washed out the remainder of the dye. A blow-dryer would have been helpful, but his hair fell smoothly into place when she combed it.

Except for his build and his striking bone structure, he scarcely resembled the man she'd seen yesterday in the alley. With his clean-shaven face and trimmed, medium-brown hair, he could have passed for a local businessman.

Well, only at first glance, she decided. On closer inspection, she didn't see how anyone could miss the wildness seething just below the surface.

"Are we done? Good." He stood and tossed aside the drape.

"Don't you want to see yourself?" She handed him a small mirror.

He spent about two seconds regarding his reflection. "It will grow back as before, will it not?"

She folded her arms. "Don't bother showering me with compliments."

"I would rather shower you with answers to our questions." He reached for a map book. "Now show me how to get to Placentia."

SHARIF CIRCLED the block twice, checking for anything out of the ordinary. Foot traffic consisted primarily of women strolling with their children alongside shops that offered jewelry, discount items and video rentals in Spanish and English. Cars, small trucks and minivans lined the curb.

"What does Griff drive?" he asked as he turned onto the block for the third time.

"Something old and rusty, as I recall." Holly sighed. "That could apply to half the vehicles here."

"Do you know if he carries a gun?"

"He's a convicted felon," she pointed out. "It would mean big trouble if he got caught."

Spotting an open space beside the curb, Sharif backed slowly to compensate for the unfamiliar bulk of the truck. "Do you believe he was innocent of the drug charge?"

"Probably, but that doesn't mean the prosecution railroaded him." Holly adjusted a strap on the used car seat that Zahad had acquired for Ben. "His pals who got convicted with him almost certainly *were* guilty."

"It was guilt by association, then. I can understand his bitterness." Behind them, a car honked, impatient at having its lane blocked.

Sharif eased the truck into the space. The idiot kept honking, as if a five-second delay posed a major imposition. When the truck's wheels straightened, the car shot past with a final, annoyed blare of the horn.

The sheikh hoped the ruckus hadn't attracted too much attention. "Stay in the truck until I come around," he said. "Take Ben out of his seat. Get ready to move quickly."

Holly didn't argue. She stayed remarkably calm under pressure, he thought.

As he swung down from the pickup, Sharif watched for any sudden movements on the street. Seeing none, he opened Holly's door and whisked her and Ben toward the restaurant.

The glass front of the building reflected a man Sharif barely recognized as himself, clean-shaven and garbed in a black leather jacket that Zahad had provided. With luck, no one would recognize him from the pictures on TV.

Inside, the place was redolent of chili peppers and spicy meat. The smoky front window and weak bulbs in wall sconces sank the place in gloom.

From a large room filled with long tables, a smaller room opened on the left. To the right, past the cashier's desk, the bar echoed with taped mariachi music.

Several of the long tables were occupied by groups of men. Sharif didn't see anyone matching Griff's description.

"Yes?" A waiter approached with frayed menus.

Holly bounced the baby on her hip. "We're meeting someone. He's short, blond, with a beard."

"This way." He took them into the room on the left, through a welter of square tables. Sharif's instincts sprang to alert as they approached a shadowed booth in the back.

The waiter stood aside. From inside the booth, a

man leaned forward until the faint light revealed a narrow face, shaggy dark-blond hair and a scraggly beard.

"Hi, Griff." Holding the baby, Holly slid onto the bench opposite the man. "How are you?"

"Not bad. Hey, you look interesting. As a brunette, I mean." After a quick, shrewd glance at Sharif, the man reached a hand across the table toward Ben. "How you doin', little man? Wanna hand him over? I think he misses me."

Sharif saw that his son was indeed gurgling and waving his arms toward the stranger. Biting back a protest, he took his seat beside Holly and allowed her to give the child to Griff.

The man tucked Ben into the crook of his arm. "You guys hungry?"

"Starving." In the narrow booth, Holly's thigh pressed against Sharif's.

"Anybody got money?"

"I have some." The sheikh kept his focus on the musician. Yet he was keenly aware of the woman next to him, and of her slightly more relaxed posture. Possibly the restaurant seemed like a safe place to her, while for him it was full of potential threats.

To the waiter, Griff instructed, "Bring us an assortment of tacos, *rellenos* and enchiladas, and three plates, okay?"

"*Si, senor.*" The man retrieved their menus and departed.

The thin man studied Sharif. "You're really a sheikh? You look more like some motorcycle dude. The upscale variety."

"Sorry to disappoint you," Sharif said.

"You wouldn't happen to be an undercover cop, by any chance?" the man asked.

"If I were, I would hardly have let her hand you a baby to use as a hostage," he replied.

"Good point. Sorry." Griff shrugged. "I get paranoid sometimes."

"I wouldn't pull a stunt like that!" Holly said, outraged. "Paranoid or not, you ought to know that. Now, are you going to answer our questions?"

"Ask away," the man said.

She leaned across the table. "Did you know Jazz was a surrogate mother?"

"Not until she camped out at my place for over a month." The man clucked at the infant in his arm. "I guess once she found out she'd been lied to, she got real closemouthed about everything."

"Lied to?" Sharif said.

The man regarded him coolly. "Yeah. About you."

BEING IN public gave Holly a sense of disorientation. How could everything seem so normal when the world had spun off its axis?

Yet she didn't feel frightened, not with Sharif at her side. Confined in the booth, he kept shifting restlessly and alternately clasped and flexed his hands atop the scarred wooden table. His energy made him seem larger than life.

"The clinic lied to her about me?" he asked Griff.

"Some guy who works there—Manuel, that's the name—said he needed to talk to her." Griff's voice took on a singsong quality. "So she met him for coffee. Or, in her case, herb tea."

"Manuel Estrellas?" Sharif asked.

"Yeah, that sounds like him." Griff clucked at

Ben. "At first, she told me she thought this guy was joking when he said the father was a sheikh. She didn't even know they existed outside of old movies."

"They did not tell her about me until she was already pregnant?" Sharif asked.

"She was a few weeks from delivering. And *they* didn't tell her anything. I guess this Manuel figured she had a right to know."

From his pocket, Sharif drew the note that Zahad had given him. "'Jazz knows,'" he read. "Apparently, this is what she knew. But who was it that called Mrs. Wheaton with this information?"

He broke off as the waiter arrived with their lunch. A platter was heaped with Mexican food, while the three plates came already half-filled by refried beans and Spanish rice.

"What are those?" The sheikh indicated one of the items on the platter.

"Stuffed chili peppers. *Relleños,*" Griff said.

"What are they stuffed with?"

"Just eat one," said the musician. "Is he always like this? I'm not trying to poison you."

Sharif scooped one onto his plate. "I apologize. Please, tell us more about Jasmine."

"She thought she was having the kid for a married couple." Griff paused to wolf down some food.

"Did she say why Manuel decided to tell her the truth?" Holly asked.

"Not that I recall." Griff helped himself to another enchilada.

Under their questioning, he told them that Jazz had refused to go to a hospital, so he'd arranged for a midwife. He'd been out of town with the band when she gave birth at home.

Afterward, she'd seemed wrapped up in the baby. As far as he knew, she hadn't had any visitors.

"Why did she send Ben to me?" Holly asked.

Griff washed down his food with a glass of water. "One day she told me she was going to meet somebody who could 'straighten things out,' that's the way she put it."

"Did she mention a name?" Sharif watched the man closely. "Noreen Wheaton, perhaps?"

"Naw. I don't even know if it was a guy or a girl," he said. "Jazz did say…" He paused, ill at ease for the first time. "She said she expected to come into some 'serious money.'"

Could Jazz have tried to blackmail the clinic director? That didn't sound like the sister Holly knew. "I can't believe she'd do anything dishonest."

"Whoever this person was, Jasmine apparently did not trust him near her son," the sheikh pointed out.

Griff nodded. "Yeah. She asked me to play babysitter. She said she was gonna pick him up in a day or so. Then she just disappeared. No note, no word about where she was going. I figured she was okay."

"What was her mood right before she left?" she asked. "Did she seem scared?"

"Not really," Griff said. "A little angry, maybe. And kind of pleased with herself. Like she'd caught somebody in the act. But what act, I don't know."

Sharif scanned the room, as he had done periodically since they sat down. "Is there anything else you can tell us?"

"Can't think of anything."

"Then we must be going. We have already stayed

longer than is safe." Sharif picked up the bill, while Holly collected the baby.

"I hope you nail the creep who did this," Griff said. "Jazz was a good friend."

"I know. Thank you for helping her. And us." Holly touched his arm gently before they left.

After paying, Sharif went outside first. A moment later, he gave the all-clear.

Holly hurried to the truck. While she strapped Ben in his seat, Sharif checked the hood and beneath the chassis. At last he vaulted into the driver's seat and locked the doors.

"What were you looking for?" she asked.

"Signs of tampering."

Fear crept along her skin. Her stiff fingers fumbled with her own seat belt.

"I doubt anyone would be so bold on such a busy street," Sharif added. "But it is a standard precaution."

That comforted her only a little. "What do we do next?"

"We need to find this clinic worker, Manuel Estrellas." The sheikh slowed, nearing a red light. "He is a link to both Jasmine and Mrs. Wheaton."

"Surely the police already…"

"Down!" As he shouted, the sheikh slammed the truck to the left. Flinging herself over Ben, Holly heard a loud crack.

The windshield. Something had hit the windshield.

# Chapter Eight

"Hang on." The truck spun sharply to the right. If Holly hadn't been wearing a seat belt, she'd have been thrown into Sharif. "Are you hurt?"

"No." Had they been set up? She couldn't believe Griff would do such a thing.

Two sharp bangs, like firecrackers, sounded ahead of them. She flinched.

"They nicked the hood." Sharif veered again. "Stay down, Holly."

"Someone's shooting at us again?" Terrorists firing at a car in broad daylight on a busy street violated her sense of order. "Why doesn't someone call the cops?"

"They probably have. I hear a siren, but it's a few blocks off," the sheikh said. "Besides, I'm not convinced the police are the best thing for us, right now."

Of course, he was right, Holly thought. Until they got more information about her sister's death, the only ones they could rely on were themselves.

Sharif yanked the truck into another sharp turn and sped forward. She braced herself for more gunfire, but heard nothing. Apparently their pursuers were having trouble getting a clear shot.

"The car windows are darkened, like yesterday," Sharif said after another check of the oversized side-view mirror. "He's gaining on us. Hang on!"

Holly gripped the edge of the seat. As the pickup shot ahead, she heard the hiss of hydraulic brakes and the hollow boom of a bus horn.

They swooped up a ramp, into the rumble of free-way traffic. Her heart thundered, and it took a while to realize that they'd settled into a steady rhythm.

"What happened?" she asked.

"A bus provided a convenient barricade," he said. "We have left the enemy behind."

Cautiously, she sat up. Her hands felt cold and damp, and she discovered she'd bitten her lip so hard it bled.

Around them surged a mixture of big rigs, vans, sport-utility vehicles and cars. To her turbulent mind, every one of them was a potential enemy. A window rolling down or a sudden lane change might presage an attack. When the pickup jounced over a pothole, Holly let out a little cry.

She wasn't sure how much more her nerves could stand. She wanted to go back to the way things used to be, when she could walk outside without watching for police cars or listening for the crack of gunfire.

"I feel like I'm living in a war zone," she said.

"In a way, you are." Sharif regarded her with concern. "You handle yourself like a trooper. Sometimes I forget that you weren't prepared for any of this."

"I want to call Trevor." She saw the tightness in his jaw, but she couldn't help herself. "Sharif, let me go home. And let me take Ben. Please."

In profile, he sat ramrod-straight. "For my son, and

for you, safety is an illusion. Even your authorities cannot guarantee it.''

''Maybe that's true in Alqedar,'' Holly said. ''It's different here. Anyway, Trevor used to be in the Marines and he's tough.''

''Tough enough to repel bullets?''

''Of course not! But—''

''You have felt safe with him in the past,'' the sheikh continued. ''Now you've been through an ordeal. It is natural to seek refuge, but also unrealistic. Your fiancé is not superhuman.''

''No, but he knows how to protect himself. And me,'' she said. ''His house has an alarm system, and it's on a hill where you can see anyone who drives up. Besides, they'd never find him, not with his phone number and address unlisted.''

''If someone traced us to the restaurant, they could certainly find out where your fiancé lives,'' the sheikh said.

She shuddered, wanting to argue further and knowing it was pointless. To her, Trevor had represented a safe harbor, and she longed to believe he still did. She wanted to believe that there was at least one place where she wouldn't have to be afraid.

The baby, who'd kept silent during the chase, began to cry. Holly wasn't sure how she could comfort him, when she couldn't even console herself.

But his lusty wail and small, earnest face brought her out of her fears and back to the present.

The baby hiccupped, his expression so startled that Holly couldn't help smiling. ''Do you think he's bored after our wild ride?''

''I am hopeful he will prefer diplomacy to the thrill

of the battlefield," Sharif said. "But he appears to have his father's love of action."

Holly tried crooning a few notes of "London Bridge Is Falling Down" to the baby in the car seat. Although she produced more quavers than tune, the fussing subsided.

The act of reassuring the baby helped her as well. For now, they'd eluded pursuit. For now, they were safe.

Studying the self-contained man at the wheel, Holly felt a calmness settle over her jangled nerves. He was just as strong as Trevor, just as capable of protecting her, and yet they were as unlike as two men could be.

Her fiancé lived by the law; Sharif broke it with abandon. He had thrust himself suddenly into Holly's life, while Trevor was her oldest friend. And where she could count on her fiancé to stay with her always, the sheikh would soon be gone.

Yet, with Sharif, she felt like a woman instead of a half-grown girl. He challenged and excited her. And scared her almost as much as the flying bullets.

She didn't want to fall in love with this fierce stranger who would soon leave and take his son with him. She had to keep her feelings in check until it was safe to go home. Yet she felt as if she were cutting off a precious part of herself.

"Someone knew where to look for us," Sharif said, half to himself. "The question is how."

He seemed to be seeking her comments. She wished she had something brilliant to offer.

Instead, thinking about the shooting gave Holly the chills again. "We could have been trapped in the restaurant. We'd have been sitting ducks."

"There must be a reason why they didn't come in," Sharif said.

"Because they're afraid of getting caught?" she ventured.

He frowned. "If it is zealots, they would not hesitate to gamble with their lives. However, if it is only one zealot, he would not take the chance of getting cornered and failing to complete his mission."

"If Griff tipped them off, maybe they had an agreement." Painful as it was, she had to explore that possibility.

"I do not think Griff was involved. He showed no signs of nervousness." Sharif angled the pickup toward a connecting freeway. "Perhaps we are on the wrong track entirely. But if it is not my enemies shooting at us, who is it?"

Holly had no answer. But she did have a new worry. "What about Griff?" she asked. "Do you think they might go after him, just because he was with us? Maybe we ought to warn him."

After brief consideration, the sheikh handed her the phone. "Be careful what you say to him. If he's assisting my enemies, he will try to find out where we're staying or to arrange another meeting."

"I'll be careful." After dialing the pager, Holly concentrated on entertaining the baby while they traced a circuitous route to the cabin. She had hoped Griff would call back immediately, but the phone remained silent.

The sky grew darker, and wind lashed the trees along the canyon road. When they reached the cabin, the eerie yellowish light intensified its air of isolation.

Sharif studied the area. "No fresh tire tracks," he said.

Holly wasn't sure how he could tell in the muddy mess. "I guess we're okay, then."

"There are other ways of reaching this place," he said. "I'm going to get out and check. Keep the motor running. If something happens to me, you must drive away."

"And leave you here? I wouldn't do that!"

The face that confronted her was stern. "You will not question my orders, Holly Rivers."

"You aren't my boss!"

On the point of arguing, Sharif caught himself. "It's true, I cannot compel you. But if this is an ambush, you cannot save me. You must save Ben. All right?"

Her stubbornness evaporated. "Yes," she whispered.

Her hands were trembling as he got out of the truck. Holly hoped she would have the fortitude to do whatever was necessary. And she hoped even more strongly that she wouldn't have to find out.

Sharif edged around the hood, watching, listening. Then he ran toward the cabin in a zigzag pattern. She held her breath, bracing for the crack of gunfire.

At the same time, the sheikh's raw courage thrilled her. He seemed to spring from another time, when a man didn't hesitate to fight for his honor or to guard his woman with his life. What would it be like to become that lady, just for one night? To bring out all the ferocity and the tenderness of which this man was capable?

Sharif unlocked the door, kicked it wide and disappeared inside. Along the lightly traveled road that ran nearby, a car speeded past, invisible behind a screen of trees but loud enough to make Holly's breath quicken.

After it passed, she almost relaxed. Then she heard another sound: the approaching rumble of a motor-cycle.

Surely, it, too, would continue on. But when it reached the turnoff, the roar grew louder. With a leap of alarm, Holly realized the biker was heading to the cabin.

She couldn't see the sheikh, and she didn't have time to free Ben and take him inside. All she could do was huddle out of sight against the baby.

Should she try to drive? The truck could outrun a bike. Unless the rider had a gun.

Or, she remembered with a start, it might be Zahad. She'd forgotten he'd switched from a car to a cycle.

Still, her heart rate didn't slow until she heard the bike engine stop. From the cabin, Sharif's voice greeted his aide.

She sat up slowly, embarrassed. She felt even worse when she discovered both men were looking at her.

"You reacted well," Zahad called.

"I did?"

"I did not even know you and the baby were there," he said. "That was excellent."

She helped Sharif unstrap Ben from the seat and walked to the cabin. Sharif filled in his aide about their meeting with Griff and the subsequent shooting attempts. "We should have waited until we could arrange for you to be in position outside the restaurant."

"I am sorry I did not respond immediately," the

man said. "Your e-mail alarmed me, but I was in the midst of receiving disturbing news from Alqedar."

"Come. We must get settled so we can give this matter our full attention."

Inside, Zahad unloaded some food supplies while Sharif brewed strong coffee. As she tended Ben, Holly couldn't help sneaking glances at the two men. Despite their similar background and blood relationship, she would never have confused the two.

An inch shorter and huskier, Zahad possessed wider cheekbones and a more agitated manner. In blue coveralls with a yellow hard hat tucked under one arm, he could pass for a construction worker. A man of many disguises, she thought.

As he dragged a chair to the table, he spoke in an impatient tenor. "President Dourad's advisers are urging that he nationalize the Jubah cloth industry immediately," he said. "They know that, for the moment, you and I are in no position to return and defend Bahrim's interests."

"How reliable are your sources?" Sharif asked.

"The report is accurate," Zahad said.

To Holly, the sheikh explained, "If our president follows this advice, the money my region generates will go into federal coffers, and little of it will reach the people of Bahrim."

His aide coughed in disgust. "Federal coffers, bah! Our money will pay for fancier offices, higher bureaucratic salaries and more 'fact-finding' tours for big shots."

"Our people need hospitals," Sharif said. "Schools. A communications infrastructure."

"Your president doesn't care about these things?" Holly held Ben against her shoulder.

"He did during the revolution," sneered Zahad. "Now he is too busy playing politics."

The sheikh poured coffee into three cups. "I do not think Abdul Dourad has been corrupted. But he must pacify a number of regional leaders, and they are greedy for our wealth."

"They should try to earn some of their own instead of stealing ours." Zahad accepted his coffee with a short nod. Holly hadn't expected the sheikh to serve his own aide, but she remembered reading that Arabs took the duties of hospitality seriously.

"Isn't there anyone in Bahrim who can stand up to these advisers?" she asked.

"At the moment, our only close associate in the country is Amy's husband, Harry Haroun." Sharif also took a seat at the table. "He's a scientist, not a statesman, and his family is not from Alqedar. Even if he speaks up, I doubt anyone will listen."

Although neither man wore traditional clothing, she could picture them in headdresses and robes sitting around a campfire. Men of their country must have conferred in this way for thousands of years, communicating with each other as much through body language as in words. Taking the measure of enemies, planning to seize power or keep what was rightfully theirs.

She had seen firsthand how swiftly and purposefully they could move. That time would no doubt come again, very soon.

"Do you think these regional leaders are behind the shootings?" she asked. "Could they be trying to kill you?"

"If they are," the sheikh said, "it would mean the disintegration of our stable government."

"It would explain a great deal, however," his cousin added. "Unlike Maimun's followers, they would have a strong motive to get rid of Sharif's son, and to cover their tracks." He turned to Holly. "As for your sister and Mrs. Wheaton, perhaps they simply knew too much."

The possibility that Jazz had been killed to eliminate her as a witness horrified Holly. What a waste of a precious life! She averted her face to hide the sheen of tears.

"There is an employee at the clinic who might be useful to us." Sharif explained to his cousin what Griff had told them about Manuel Estrellas.

"Unless he also has disappeared, I am sure the police have talked to him," Zahad responded. "But they might not have asked the right questions."

"If you can believe Griff, and I do, this Manuel was honest with my sister," Holly said. "He might be willing to talk to us, too."

Sharif agreed. "Small details and impressions that the police would dismiss as irrelevant might mean something to us."

His phone rang. It was Griff.

"We want to warn you that we were fired on when we left the restaurant," Sharif said. "Yes? Good idea."

As Zahad listened, his face betrayed no expression. The aide certainly played his cards close to his chest, Holly thought. She might have wondered about his trustworthiness, except that Sharif knew his cousin at least as well as she knew Trevor.

The sheikh hung up. "After we left the restaurant, he heard a lot of sirens. He suggests we watch the news to see if anyone was captured. He himself plans to go into hiding for a while."

Holly remembered the sheikh's earlier warning. "He didn't ask where we are or try to set up a meeting?" He shook his head. "I knew he was innocent!"

"It is good advice about the news. Perhaps some camera will give us a glimpse of these attackers." Zahad went to turn on the TV.

First up was a report of a severe storm moving in. Meteorologists expected it to hit the area later that afternoon. Then an anchorwoman replaced the forecaster on screen.

"Police in Placentia are investigating reports of shots fired from a moving car, possibly at another vehicle, about half an hour ago," she said. "No arrests have been made and officers wouldn't say whether they believe the incident was gang-related."

Sharif leaned over Holly to cup the back of his son's head in his hand. "Apparently the news media, at least, do not connect us with this business."

"How convenient to have activities reported so quickly on TV," Zahad said dryly. "I suspect the criminals appreciate it also."

"Considering the way our crime rate's been dropping in the past few years, this can't be helping them," Holly replied.

"That is because your police are wise enough not to tell the press much," returned the aide. "And why does the station let this blond woman read the news? She appears better suited to describing the latest fashions!"

It seemed to Holly that he was deliberately provoking her by making such a chauvinist remark. "If light-colored hair makes a person stupid, then my IQ must have risen twenty points since this morning. Don't you agree?''

For the first time that she could recall, the man smiled. ''I am beginning to like this woman,'' he told the sheikh. ''She has a quick mind, but an even temper. Amy could take lessons from her.''

Sharif chuckled as he caressed Ben's little cheek. His hand brushed Holly's shoulder, and she felt as if he were stroking her as well. ''My two cousins have a friendly rivalry.''

''Not always so friendly,'' Zahad said. ''Her tongue is dipped in acid.''

''That sounds painful.'' Holly feigned dismay. ''Although I'm not sure for which one of you.''

''Wait!'' The sheikh stared at the screen. ''More news, and it concerns us.''

A male reporter was interviewing a graying man in a white coat. ''This is Dr. Albert Lowrie, the obstetrician who treated murder victim Hannah Jasmine Rivers during her pregnancy. Dr. Lowrie, you're a partner in the Crestline View Clinic. Do you think there's any connection between Ms. Rivers's death and Noreen Wheaton's disappearance?''

''I can't imagine why there would be.'' The man had a pudgy face and shadowed eyes. ''I just hope Noreen's all right.''

''A clinic employee has indicated that Ms. Rivers might not have been aware that Sheikh Al-Khalil was the father of her baby,'' the man continued. ''Was she tricked into bearing his child?''

Dr. Lowrie ran a hand through his thinning hair. ''Not to my knowledge. You have to understand, I spend only a few hours a week at the clinic. Most of my work is done in my office in Newport Beach and at the hospital where I'm affiliated. The surrogacy patients are a small part of my caseload.''

"How are the surrogates recruited?'' the man asked.

"Mrs. Wheaton handles that department,'' said the doctor. "I believe she advertises discreetly. Sometimes women contact us and volunteer to give the gift of life.''

"And are they screened for emotional stability?''

"Of course!'' he said. "We run a complete medical and psychological evaluation.''

"Thank you, Dr. Lowrie. Now, back to…''

Holly laid the baby down for a nap. "That man's name rings a bell.''

"The doctor?'' Sharif laid a spare blanket gently across his son. He stood so close to Holly that his body carved a space around hers. Their legs touched, nearly entwining for an instant before he drew away.

She struggled to get back to the point. "Yes, the doctor. Alice recommended him for my annual checkup. I decided he was too expensive, though, so I went to a clinic instead.''

"Alice?'' said Zahad from across the room. "Ah yes, that would be your employer, Mrs. Frey. We saw her at the church.''

They must have been observing the courtyard for some time before they snatched Ben. It was an unsettling thought. Holly had always assumed she would know at some level if she were being watched.

"So Alice is one of his patients?'' Sharif said. "It is quite a coincidence.''

"Not really,'' Holly said. "I mean, he's very prominent. Someone in my apartment building had recommended him, too.''

"Perhaps Mrs. Frey suggested that Jasmine consult him," added the aide. "He might be the one who suggested that she become a surrogate."

"It is a possible link," the sheikh agreed. "Do you think your employer would remember?"

"Probably." Holly took a swallow of the coffee he'd left for her. "I should call her again anyway. She'll be worried about Ben."

"It's too dangerous to keep telephoning her," Zahad said. "Does she have e-mail?"

"Probably, but I don't know her address."

"Give me yours," said the aide. "I will try to contact this woman and ask that she get in touch."

"You're going to see Alice?"

"I would like to observe the salon and its comings and goings, anyway," he said. "Who knows what information might turn up?"

It sounded like a far-fetched idea, but Zahad regarded her steadily and Sharif made no objection. If he trusted his aide's judgment, Holly decided as she scribbled her little-used e-mail address on a pad, then so did she.

"Also, I will do some checking on Mr. Estrellas," Zahad said.

"Do not approach him directly," Sharif said.

His cousin gave him a ghost of a smile. "I assure you, I have no intention of it. He will be much more likely to talk to Ms. Rivers than to either of us."

"This matter will go more quickly if we divide the tasks." Sharif stood and briskly collected the coffee cups. "I can leave Holly and Ben here for a while."

"No!" the aide said.

His abrupt tone was met with a raised eyebrow. "You are giving me orders?" said the sheikh.

"Of course not." The man made a conciliatory gesture. "However, we cannot leave your son unprotected. Also, from here you can track developments in Alqedar on the Internet. I have barely skimmed the surface, and probably missed many subtleties. You are far more knowledgeable about business matters than I."

A muscle jumped in the sheikh's jaw. Frustration, Holly thought. "Very well," he said reluctantly. "Today, you can be the warrior. But if you need assistance, you will call me. At once!"

"I understand." Zahad clasped his cousin's hand and said something in a foreign language.

Sharif's lips pressed tightly. Holly could have sworn he was holding back tears.

After Zahad drove off, she ventured, "What did he say to you?"

"That we are closer than brothers. It is true." Although it was only midafternoon, the room had gone nearly dark. When the sheikh switched on the lamp, a golden glow bathed them. "I plan to follow his advice. Will you come with me as we prowl through cyberspace?"

"You make it sound like an adventure."

"It can be. Or a massive waste of time." He smiled and placed a chair beside him, then opened his laptop.

The prospect of sitting so close to him kindled a disturbing heat inside Holly. Wrapping her arms around herself, she hesitated.

"Have I offended you?" His dark gaze fixed on her face.

"No. Why?"

"It seems you do not wish for my company." His teasing baritone sent mellow vibrations through her.

''It's not that, but the chairs are so close. And when you touch me...'' She hesitated.

''You feel it also?'' he murmured.

''Nothing can come of it,'' Holly said.

''And nothing will,'' he replied. ''I am not a casual seducer of women.'' She might have felt reassured, except that he added, ''However, with you, nothing would be casual.''

''What do you mean by that?''

''I wish I knew what I meant.'' Sharif sighed. ''Do you know, Holly Rivers, you confuse me more than any other woman?''

''I can't imagine anything confusing you. You're so strong.''

His rough fingers tapped restlessly near the keyboard. ''I, too, understand that we must not become close. And yet I wish to enjoy these few hours that we share. It makes no sense for you to sit across the room when you could be here beside me.''

Suddenly she felt foolish. Why was she making such a big deal about sitting next to a man?

So what if his nearness sent a river of heat through her blood? All the more reason to relish this unexpected friendship—even for the little time they had.

Resolutely, she sat down. Together, they paged through gossip, news and speculation from Alqedar, much of it contradictory.

Once, Sharif reached toward Holly's sweep of hair. She froze, half alarmed but half hoping he would touch her in some new way. But all he did was tuck an errant strand behind her ear.

True to his word, Holly acknowledged, Sharif was not a seducer of women.

She was surprised at how little the discovery pleased her.

# *Chapter Nine*

From a phone booth at a gas station, Zahad called the clinic. His first step was to determine whether Manuel Estrellas had been taken into police custody and was, therefore, out of their reach.

"Crestline View," a female voice answered.

"Manuel Estrellas, please." A diesel truck lumbered into the station, drowning her response. "Excuse me?"

"I said, he doesn't work here anymore."

"Can you tell me where to reach him?" He wondered whether the police were already tracing the call. Surely they couldn't track every inquiry that came into the medical clinic.

"I'm sorry, I can't give out his home address or phone number," the woman said.

He ought to hang up. But caution had never been Zahad's style. "Does he have an e-mail address or another work number, by any chance?"

There was a pause. Was she alerting someone? "May I ask what this concerns?"

He had prepared a story, of course. "My name is Mitchell Kahn. I was talking to Mr. Estrellas about buying some life insurance."

"Life insurance? That's funny," she said. "He isn't married or anything. Oh, can I put you on hold?"

"No, thanks." He hung up and hurried to his motorcycle. If the police were on their way, Zahad didn't intend to stick around and wait for them.

He'd already checked the phone book to make sure there was no listing under the name Manuel Estrellas. The only other possible connection to the man was Dr. Lowrie, but the physician would be even more unlikely than the receptionist to reveal anything.

Alice Frey might prove a useful connection, or a dangerous one. Her involvement with the doctor aroused Zahad's suspicions. He preferred to deal with her himself and keep her away from Holly and Sharif.

He set a course for the Sunshine Lane Salon. Earlier today, when he swung by for reconnaissance, he'd determined that there was road work going on nearby. Hence the blue coveralls and the hard hat.

As he drove, he kept watch for any suspicious vehicle. Because it was legal here for a motorcycle to zip between lanes of traffic, he moved in such a deliberately erratic manner that any car trying to keep pace would call attention to itself. None did.

On the bike, he went through a fast-food drive-in line and picked up a chicken sandwich. A construction worker eating a late lunch would attract less attention than a man loitering.

The beauty shop was located in a string of small businesses, whose shared parking lot was half-full. Between the small center and a supermarket lay a modest park. Along with a playground and a few wooden picnic tables, it offered a partial view of the salon.

On the far side of the street sprawled a light industrial park. In front of it, construction work blocked a lane of traffic.

As he'd told Sharif and Holly, Zahad wanted to see who visited Alice and who might be conducting surveillance on her. If he saw nothing disturbing, he would watch for an opportunity to approach her directly.

Overhead, storm clouds bulked. As he parked behind the grassy area, Zahad wondered how soon the rain would start.

The ominous weather created one advantage. It had discouraged anyone else from using the park.

He checked his watch. 1:37 p.m.

The chicken sandwich was greasy, but he'd long ago schooled himself not to notice what went into his stomach. A man in his position couldn't waste time on niceties.

In front of the salon, a station wagon bearing the name of a beauty supply company pulled into a slot. A young man carried a black sample case inside. Zahad wondered how well the beauticians knew these salespeople, and whether he might be able to sneak inside in such a guise.

A while later, the man exited. He was followed out of the building by a middle-aged woman, her puffy hair tinted the color of champagne.

As she drove away, a Lexus arrived. The woman who emerged wore a scarf and carried a wig on a mannequin head.

Zahad finished his sandwich. On the street, the workmen were collecting their orange cones.

When they left, he would need to go, also. At least

he'd be able to get rid of this hat, which, despite the breeze, made his head sweat.

Removing it, he shook back his hair. As he did, another woman came out of the salon. Short and stocky, with gray-dappled brown hair. Alice.

Trying to look casual, Zahad replaced his hat and watched her from the corner of his eye. If she got in her car, he decided to follow.

Instead, however, she headed in his direction along the sidewalk. The path would carry her to within a dozen feet of him.

Where was she going? To the supermarket, or to meet someone?

From his pocket, Zahad retrieved the copy of Holly's e-mail address. He would seize this opportunity, and then beat a rapid retreat. Shifting his balance, he started to rise when he glimpsed a movement on the street.

It was a police cruiser, coming abreast. Slowly, he sank onto his picnic bench.

The police car stopped at the curb. The cop, who was solo, lowered the passenger window. "Mrs. Frey?"

She stopped. "Oh, hello, Officer Williams."

"I was coming to check on you. Everything all right?"

"I'm just going to get some sandwiches at the supermarket deli. Most of us don't get to eat until after the lunch crush." Zahad didn't dare look up, but her voice sounded strained.

"Nothing happening? No weird calls, visitors, etc.?"

"We're all fine."

The rest of the conversation was lost as a group of

cars and trucks went by. Finally Alice continued on her way.

By the time the cruiser merged into traffic, she'd passed the rim of the park. Zahad would have to catch her on the way back.

At least he'd learned that the salon wasn't being staked out. And evidently she hadn't blabbed about hearing from Holly. If she had, the cops would be showing a lot more interest.

The road crew loaded their gear into a truck. Zahad knew he couldn't stay here much longer. How long did it take to get sandwiches from a deli counter, anyway?

Impatiently, he carried his trash to a receptacle. It was nearly three o'clock, and moisture laced the chill breeze.

"Zahad Adran. Did I pronounce that correctly?"

The words startled him into scraping his hand on the edge of the trash can. He turned sharply.

Alice Frey stood about four feet away. She must have cut through the back of the park instead of going into the supermarket.

He pretended to be confused. "I am sorry. I don't know who you mean."

"I recognized you from your photograph." She studied him with steely determination. "It's the hair. I saw it when you took off your hat. Straight and ragged, and such a coarse texture. We don't see much of that around here."

Before he could respond, a movement on the street caught his attention. The police cruiser. It must have circled the block and come back.

Keeping his hand out of the officer's line of sight,

Zahad slipped it inside his jacket. This time, he had brought a gun.

OUT OF THE corner of his eye, Sharif watched Holly stretch in her chair. The sight of her pleasing curves provided a welcome relief after his frustrating discovery on the Internet.

He had learned that on Thursday, the day after tomorrow, a bill would be entered in Alqedar's parliament to nationalize regional industries. The timing couldn't be a coincidence. Although such a bill might have been in the works, someone was taking advantage of the sheikh's absence.

He must hurry back, yet it might be dangerous to return. And, after sitting beside Holly for the past hour, he found himself reluctant to think of leaving.

An awareness of her filled his senses. The pearly curve of her ear, the scent of her hair and the dewiness of her cheek seemed to invite his touch. Even the tension of holding himself in check reminded Sharif that he was all male.

She stood and wrapped her arms around herself. "Are you cold?" he asked.

Her startled gaze met his, and he read the answer in her dilated pupils and parted lips. It wasn't a chill that made her react, but a need to stem her reaction to him.

"It is a bit cool in here," she said.

"I'll build a fire."

"That isn't necessary."

"I don't mind." Eager to occupy his body with something other than fantasies about Holly, Sharif paced to the hearth. He selected sticks of firewood from a curved metal carrier and laid them in a pattern.

Holly came to stand beside the hearth. "Are you trying to get away from me?"

"What makes you ask such a question?" he demanded, keeping his gaze on the firewood. "We've just spent an hour in each other's company."

"We've just spent an hour avoiding each other's gazes, and it's been hard work, hasn't it?" she said. "The minute I stood up, you scampered over here as if a demon were chasing you."

"I do not scamper," said the sheikh.

"You're avoiding the issue." She watched him steadily.

"Perhaps I was mistaken to ask you to sit by me," Sharif conceded as he worked. "In my country, a man would never spend time alone with an unmarried woman, especially not one wearing such revealing clothes."

"What's revealing about them?" Holly indicated the shirt and jeans Zahad had provided. "Everybody dresses this way."

"Not everyone has breasts that lift the fabric with every inhalation," he said, standing and examining her frankly. "Or hips so slim that the jeans slip down and bare your navel."

As his gaze traced this tempting sight, he couldn't resist the urge to clasp his hands around the bare flesh of her waist. She trembled beneath his touch but didn't draw back.

His thumbs traced the hollow of her rib cage and gently circled her navel. Holly swayed toward him. Through the shirt, he could see the nipples spring erect, and her face tilted upward, ready for his kiss.

Should he take her now? He doubted she would

refuse him. To make love would satisfy this swelling need in them both, and ease his mind and spirit.

With every inviting look, with every shuddering breath, Holly offered herself to him. A warrior was entitled to take whatever a woman gave freely. Why should he care that she was going to marry another man?

But could he mate with her and walk away unchanged? In making love, he would be giving her a part of himself. When she was gone, could he honestly believe that he would feel no loss?

Ruefully, Sharif acknowledged that he did not know himself as well as he had believed. This vulnerability to Holly might extend far beyond these few hours in this isolated cabin. He could not afford the distraction from his people and his duty. Nor did he wish to cause her any injury.

"We must not pursue a flirtation." He turned away and busied himself positioning wood chips around the logs as kindling.

"Why?" Holly asked. "A moment ago, you couldn't keep your hands off me."

"You're a very tempting woman."

"Not so tempting you can't resist me, obviously." She sounded hurt.

Sharif refused to discuss his own uncertainties. Instead, he flared, "I have known the deepest love a man and a woman can experience. Once in a lifetime is enough."

She fell silent, her eyelids lowered. Was she angry? Sharif wasn't sure. Or might she be contemplating her own feelings for Trevor?

As he retrieved a box of matches, she said, "Your

wife must have been a very special woman. How did you two meet?''

''It was an arranged marriage.'' Sharif tossed a match into the kindling.

''Arranged?'' Her voice sounded tremulous. ''How long before the wedding did you meet?''

''Three days,'' he said.

''Three...days?''

''I was twenty-two and had just graduated from college. My uncle, Amy's father, chose my wife. After my parents were killed, he became my second father and head of our tribe, although under the dictatorship he could wield no real power.''

''Is he still alive?''

''Sadly, he died during the revolution, after years of poor health,'' Sharif said. ''But he did me the great favor of choosing the right woman for me to marry.''

''You didn't object?'' she asked. ''Either you or your bride?''

''Of course not. We shared the same goal, the liberation of our country,'' he said. ''Yona came to join me at the camp where Zahad and I were training in North Africa. We knew very soon that we would be happy together.''

''What if you hadn't liked her?'' Holly asked.

''I would have married her anyway,'' Sharif said. ''To do otherwise would have brought shame on my family and hers.''

''I could never do anything like that!'' she said.

The match died without sparking a fire. He lit another and, instead of tossing it, slid it into place. The flame licked toward his fingers, and he released it at the last possible moment.

''Was your marriage not also arranged for practical

considerations?'' he said. ''Your groom is older and well established in business. You can hardly pretend that your emotions have run away with you.''

''But he isn't a stranger,'' she pointed out. ''He's a friend, someone I know I can rely on. As long as I can remember, Trevor's been there for me and Jazz.''

The wood caught fire at last. ''I did not realize you had known him for such a long time.''

''Trevor and my father were best friends ever since they served together in the military.'' Still hugging her knees, Holly let the fireglow bathe her face.

''So he was like an uncle to you?'' Such an intimate connection indicated a deeper bond between these two than Sharif had suspected. Although not superficially romantic, it might in time produce a satisfying marriage.

''He was more than that. When I was fifteen, Dad smashed his car into a tree. He had a drinking problem, you see.'' Holly's expression grew distant, as if she were watching an old movie that only she could see. ''Three years later, Mom died of cancer. I don't know what we would have done without Trevor.''

''Your sister must have been a minor at the time,'' Sharif said. ''Who raised her?''

''I did,'' Holly said. ''Trevor helped out, whenever she got too wild. He was the executor of our parents' estate, not that there was much of an estate to execute.''

''Your parents didn't have insurance?'' His admiration grew, for this woman who had taken responsibility for her sister at such a young age.

She shrugged. ''No, and Mom had used up their savings on medical bills. They didn't even own a house, just a piece of land about fifty miles from here, in the middle of nowhere. Dad won it in a poker game, I think. Trevor rented it to some hermit types who live in a mobile home.''

''What did you live on?'' he asked.

''Social Security survivors' benefits, plus I worked part-time while I was going to beauty school,'' she said. ''Trevor and his wife helped out, too. I'm sure the money came out of their own pockets.''

''His wife?'' Sharif hadn't known of the man's previous marriage.

''We used to call her Aunt Karen.'' Holly stretched her hands toward the flames. ''They got divorced about five years ago. Trevor said they just drifted apart.''

''This woman accepts your marriage to her former husband?'' Such a romantic tangle might easily occur in one of the large households in Bahrim, Sharif reflected. His aunt Selima claimed no soap opera could compare.

''Karen remarried and moved east a couple of years ago,'' she said. ''We lost contact.''

The phone rang. It was about time he heard from Zahad, the sheikh thought, although he was sorry to break off this quiet interchange with Holly. ''Yes?''

''This accursed weather!'' Amy spoke tartly in their native tongue. ''Can you believe I'm stuck in Chicago in a snowstorm? I can't get to Los Angeles until tomorrow.''

''Be careful. There are gunmen looking for me.'' He considered warning her not to come, but then who would take the baby?

''I will be on my guard, as always.'' His cousin had undergone extensive security training. ''Our first step must be to get you a lawyer so you can stop skulking around in the bushes, or wherever you are. Have you heard what Parliament is trying to pull off?''

''They want to steal our factory.'' He heard the hardness in his own voice. ''We must stop them, one way or another. They are betraying everything we fought for in Alqedar's revolution.''

''Of course. Besides, they're not only greedy, they're incompetent,'' she said. ''Within a year, the industry will be riddled with corruption. I have instructed Harry to get out of his laboratory and speak on television, but heaven knows what he will say.''

The prospect of bashful Harry in his white lab coat trying to debate with some silver-tongued politician was daunting. ''Catch the first flight you can,'' Sharif said. ''I don't care how much the lawyer costs, as long as he can send me home.''

Behind Amy, an airport loudspeaker made an announcement too garbled to comprehend, and she waited until it ended. ''I have a list of firms in Los Angeles, the ones who have handled the big trials,'' his cousin said when she could make herself heard. ''They will do a good job.''

''They will call press conferences and make much of themselves!'' Sharif had little patience with public relations, which was why he let Amy handle such matters for their province. ''I do not want to be tried in the media.''

''Do you have a better suggestion?'' she asked. ''Listen, I have to go check whether that announcement was for me. I will call when I know more, all right?''

''Yes, of course. Thank you, Amy. And be careful.'' Sharif clicked off the phone.

Through the slanted blinds, he could see a leaden sky. But it wasn't nearly as dark as the future of Bahrim would be if his people were robbed of their economic security.

His deep ache for Holly, his concern over Jazz's death, none of this mattered. Despite the possibility of walking into a trap, he and Ben must go home as soon as possible, which meant he must secure an attorney on his own. Who knew how long Amy might be held up?

"I need a criminal lawyer," he said. "Do you have any suggestions?"

"Trevor mostly handles civil contracts but he's active in the bar association. I'm sure he knows someone." Rising to her feet, Holly dusted off her jeans.

"Someone good enough to get me released on bail?" he said.

"I can ask." She hesitated. "You really want me to call him?"

"Do you object?"

"No, I guess not. But isn't his phone likely to be tapped?"

"We have to assume so. You know his cell phone number?"

"Yes. No." Her cheeks flushed. "I should, shouldn't I? But he got a new one last month and I haven't memorized it."

Sharif weighed the possibility of simply choosing a lawyer from the phone book. No; he needed the best. Besides, from what Holly had told him, Trevor deserved to be reassured about her well-being.

"Here is what we must do," he said. "You will call him, but not from here. Take the truck and go to a pay phone at least five miles away." Resolutely,

Sharif squelched his own misgivings. "I will stay with Ben."

Dark hair tangled around her startled face. "You want me to go out alone?"

There was a slim chance his enemies might spot the pickup, but he considered it unlikely. Also, for his country's sake, he couldn't gamble on being arrested now.

"By yourself, you are less likely to be noticed," he said. "Together, you, me and Ben are rather obvious, don't you think?"

"All right," she said. "I'll go if you think I should."

"Yes," he said. "It is necessary."

THE POLICE car swung to the curb. Keeping one hand inside his jacket, Zahad considered whether he should shove past Alice and make a break for the motorcycle.

In that moment of indecision, he heard the cop call, "Hey, Mrs. Frey, you all right? This guy bothering you?"

"No, no, we're old friends," she said. "What's up, Officer Williams?"

"I forgot to ask you something. For my wife's birthday, I want to give her a, you know, a beauty makeover. Does your salon have a package like that?"

"Of course." Alice betrayed no sign of nerves. "Just call me and we'll set the whole thing up."

"Great. Thanks!" With a wave, he drove off.

Zahad didn't relax until the cruiser was out of sight. When he turned to Alice, she folded her arms and pierced him with a stare. "All right, Mr. Adran. What have you done with my baby?"

"*Your* baby?"

"Ben Rivers is as close to a grandchild as I'm likely to get, given that my son shows no inclination to get married." The woman was half Zahad's size and a good fifteen years his elder, but she confronted him without fear. "Where is he? And where's Holly?"

"They are both safe." Raindrops began to patter on his hard hat. "Is it all right if we step out of this rain?"

"Fine. But don't think I'm letting you off the hook." She headed for a roofed barbecue site so fast that Zahad's long legs had to take extra strides to catch up with her short ones.

At the shelter, Alice executed a quick, expert fluff of her silver-laced brown hair. "This place dry enough for you?" she said. "Good. Now, why were you watching me?"

He handed her Holly's e-mail address. "She wants you to contact her. The phones are becoming too dangerous."

Clear gray eyes scrutinized him. "Why is she co-operating with you? What have you done to her?"

"I assure you, despite our actions, we are not criminals," Zahad said. "Sheikh Al-Khalil was only reclaiming his own son, as is his right."

"Ben's an American," Alice said. "He belongs here."

"If you want to debate custody, talk to a lawyer." Zahad pressed on. "Griff Goldbar says that Jasmine was tricked into becoming a surrogate. We need to reach a man who used to work at the clinic, Manuel Estrellas. Do you know him?"

"Why do you think I would?"

"Because you are the person who referred her to Dr. Lowrie." He didn't actually know that that was true, but it was a reasonable inference.

The salon owner took an instinctive step backward. It was the first time she'd shown any sign of being intimidated. "Look, I just want Ben to stay in this country. I'm not involved in this clinic business."

"You sent Jazz to that doctor."

"I don't think she ever actually saw him for a checkup!" Alice protested. "Lots of people make referrals. That doesn't mean I'm responsible for unforeseen consequences."

"Like murder?" he said.

She started. "I resent your implication!"

He'd gone too far, Zahad realized. He didn't mean to antagonize her. "Then I apologize. Please. We need your help."

Her gaze met his, squarely. "I want to find out who killed Jazz, and that's the only reason I'm going to help you, Mr. Adran. Dr. Lowrie's nurse is one of my customers. I can nose around."

"Thank you."

"I'll even throw in a free haircut when this is over," she added. "You need one."

He couldn't help smiling. There was something appealing about this strong-willed woman, who was, after all, only trying to protect a beloved child. His own mother had stood up for him until she died, much too young.

"I am sorry you cannot keep this boy," he said. "But it is your son, not my sheikh, who owes you grandchildren."

"He suffers from what we call a fear of commitment." Alice sighed.

"In Alqedar, the elders arrange marriages for men like him."

"I doubt he'd go for it." She eyed Zahad shrewdly. "What about you? Are you married?"

"Well, no."

"Why haven't they leg-shackled you yet?"

He saw no point in evasiveness. "My father lives in Germany with my stepmother. He has declared her eldest son, my younger half brother, as his heir. No one cares whether I get married."

"You're not bad-looking," Alice said. "You could find a wife on your own, once you have a decent haircut."

"We look forward to receiving any information you can unearth about this man Estrellas," he said, not bothering to dignify her last comment with a response. With a terse nod of farewell, Zahad dashed into the thickening rain.

He had much to do. There was no more time to waste on women who pined for grandchildren and prattled of romance.

THE MINUTE the pickup pulled out of the clearing, Sharif knew he should never have allowed Holly to take such a risk. He also knew that it was only his fear that told him so.

In any case, there was no way to stop her now. She had taken a cloned phone in case of an emergency, but he couldn't call her on a stolen number.

On the bed, the baby was still dozing. With each passing hour, Sharif noticed more details about him. How could anyone miss the auburn highlights in his dark hair, and the way his little mouth pursed?

Minutes ticked by. Which direction had Holly

gone? How could he be sure the assassins wouldn't spot her, when he didn't know how they'd managed to locate him in the past?

Craving action, hemmed in by four walls and a heavy sense of responsibility, Sharif grabbed the remote and switched channels. He was tired of seeing the same pictures, over and over, of himself and Zahad.

There! Seeing Amy's husband on CNN, he upped the volume.

"People around the world are just beginning to realize how wonderful Jubah cloth is." Although Harry wore his customary wire-rimmed glasses, he stood up straighter than usual in a silky, tailored suit. No doubt Selima had selected it. "The synthetic is chemically indistinguishable from the natural form."

"Mr. Haroun," the interviewer said, "do you think this attempt to nationalize your industry is timed to take advantage of Sheikh Al-Khalil's fugitive status?"

"Of course it is!" Harry blinked as if taken aback by his own forcefulness. "My wife and I aren't going to sit by and let our people get trampled."

"Realistically, is there anything you can do to stop this encroachment?" the man said.

"We want to remind President Dourad that he still needs Bahrim's support to maintain his coalition." Harry spoke with more confidence now. "We are, you might say, hanging tough."

"Good for you!" Sharif said aloud, glad to see his cousin's husband rising to the occasion.

His exhilaration was short-lived. The slap of rain against the roof brought him back to the cabin and to the reality that Holly was out there driving in this downpour, on her way to telephone the man she planned to marry.

According to his watch, it was 3:20 p.m. She should be back by four.

There would still be time for him to call a lawyer today. If everything went well.

# Chapter Ten

Trevor's secretary put Holly through to him at once. "Thank heaven you're all right!" were his first words. "Where are you?"

His familiar voice made it hard to believe that the events of the past twenty-four hours were real. Although she'd only driven out of the canyon and underneath the freeway to this phone booth by a coffee shop, Holly felt as if she'd transitioned from one world to another.

But in which one did she belong?

"I can't tell you where I am," she said.

"Yes, you can. I'm coming to get you." His tone brooked no argument, but she gave him one, anyway.

"No, you're not. I have to stay and take care of the baby." Outside the phone booth, the drizzle thickened into rain.

"You have to what? The man's playing mind games with you!"

"Sharif is innocent," Holly protested. "He didn't hurt Jazz."

"He's manipulating you, honey." She could picture Trevor sitting in the swivel chair behind his mahogany desk, running his hand through his short-cropped blond hair until it stood straight up. "The guy's real slick. I've been reading up on him. You can't trust him."

She refused to be sidetracked. "Is this phone tapped?"

"It better not be. I get privileged communications from my clients on this line," Trevor said. "Which I'm sure that sheikh took into account when he told you to call me here."

"Look, nobody's holding a gun to my head," she said. "I'm here all by myself."

"Okay, okay." She heard the creak of his chair as he leaned back. "Tell me what I need to do to get you back."

"Give me the name of a criminal attorney." The rain was coming down harder by the second. "The best one you know."

"For—him?" he asked.

It *did* sound crazy, asking her fiancé to help the man who'd abducted her, she supposed. "Once he comes out in the open, so can I."

"Then he *is* holding you prisoner!"

"Trevor, please stop trying to second-guess me!" Her frustration stemmed as much from her own nagging sense of guilt as from his stubbornness, she realized. "Just help me on this one, okay?"

"Well, let me look through my address book. A criminal attorney, huh?"

"That's right. A good one."

Seconds ticked by. Outside, water sheeted around the phone booth. This was taking too long, she thought, and then the truth hit.

Trevor was prolonging this call on purpose. He'd

betrayed her, even though he probably thought he was saving her.

"You've signaled the police!" She might already be trapped. How long did it take to trace a call? How soon would they arrive? "I'm hanging up!"

"Holly, I'm sorry! Call Edward Hoolihan." The name reached her in the split second before she hung up.

How naive she'd been, not to consider that Trevor might prearrange with the police to trace one specific call! Now she had to get out of here, fast.

Her heart pounding, Holly peered through the rain. She saw no flashing red lights, not yet.

Beyond the truck, which she'd left close to the phone booth, she spotted a couple of cars huddled in front of the restaurant. On the road, other vehicles swished by and disappeared into the downpour.

Keeping her head low, she dashed to the pickup. As she got in, she saw a blond woman emerge from the restaurant. To her relief, the woman was too absorbed in dodging toward her sport-utility vehicle to notice Holly.

When the truck engine sputtered to life, every instinct screamed at her to hurry. She gripped the wheel, reminding herself that she wasn't used to driving such a large vehicle. The last thing she needed was a collision, with the SUV or anything else.

Eons ticked by as she eased away from the phone booth. At the curb, she grumbled in frustration as she waited for a break in traffic.

A red sports car zipped into the parking lot, its speakers booming. In her side-view mirror, Holly saw brake lights flash as the SUV nearly backed into the newcomer.

Ahead of her, a traffic break opened at last. The pickup rumbled onto the street, jouncing over the curb cut so roughly that it jarred Holly's spine.

With the windshield wipers fighting a losing battle against the rain, it took all her concentration to stay in her lane. She'd driven less than a block when a red light flashed toward her in the opposite lane. Holly flinched as a siren shrilled past.

The police had arrived. She'd been right about Trevor.

---

IT WAS THREE minutes before four o'clock. Sharif no longer needed to check his watch; his mind was counting the seconds.

He had fed and changed the baby and played tickle games with him. Now the crackling fire had lulled Ben back to sleep.

Gently, the sheikh adjusted the covers around his son, who slept in the large wicker basket. The sleeping infant, the fire and the thrum of rain all created a cozy scene, but it did nothing to ease his restlessness.

What was taking Holly so long?

In the charged atmosphere she'd left behind, her lingering perfume summoned ghostly memories. Everywhere Sharif looked, he saw her sitting, stretching, brushing her hair, smiling at him.

The partly open closet revealed the wedding dress Holly had worn the previous day. The dress that she'd planned to take off last night, for another man. The man whom she'd gone to call.

If she changed her mind and returned to her old life, he would understand. He'd had no right to disrupt her plans. He had no right to demand anything, to expect anything.

Yet every inch of Sharif's being vibrated with his need for her. He would not, could not let her go. When had his heart turned traitor? When had he developed this sense that she bound up the raw edges of his life?

Through the front window, he stared into a world turned to water. Waves of it bent the trees until they seemed to kneel in surrender.

Headlights glimmered, distorted by the storm. Someone was coming. Who?

HOLLY'S EYES burned from squinting to see the road. Fear became so pervasive that she could feel herself dissolving into it.

Three police cruisers had swooped by her toward the restaurant lot. Burned into her retinas was the scene she'd glimpsed in her side-view mirror, of officers surrounding the SUV and the sports car. They must have believed the blond woman was her.

What kept her steady the whole way home was the sense that Sharif was with her. Compared to his presence in her heart, everything and everyone else faded.

Including Trevor.

She couldn't be angry at her fiancé, who had done what he believed was best. He had no reason to doubt that she cared for him as she had a few days before. The truth was that, at this moment, she could scarcely remember what he looked like.

A swivel of the wheel, a couple of thumps and she halted in front of the cabin. She was home.

For a dazed moment, Holly couldn't find the energy to move. Then the heavy wash of rain across the windshield eased, as if the storm were taking a breath.

In that brief remission, she jumped from the truck and raced to the cabin.

She desperately needed Sharif's solid support and his mouth against hers. Then the door flung open, and he was there.

Holly hurtled against him, and he wrapped her inside his strength. Joy sparkled through her veins as she curved against him.

"They nearly caught me." The words spilled out. "Trevor had the call traced."

"You are all right?" Close to her ear, his baritone skimmed directly into her brain.

"Yes. Now that I'm with you."

As their mouths met, the sheikh's exotic scent enveloped her and, through his clothing, she felt his muscles tighten. Eagerly, she ran her hands across his arms and shoulders, relishing the man's sheer masculine perfection.

He lifted his head. In the flickering light, his eyes burned into hers, and then he bent over her again.

Slowly, sensuously, Sharif's lips grazed her throat and found the pulse. From her waistband, his hands moved upward, lifting her shirt, closing over her breasts. A groan tore from him, as if desire had at long last ripped away all constraints.

Fire raced through Holly. She made one last, futile attempt to marshal her defenses, but then he caught the tips of her breasts in his mouth, one after the other in fierce succession, and she was lost.

"Come." The sheikh led her through the lamplight into the shadows of the alcove. Holly wasn't sure she was ready for what was about to happen, and yet she could not step even one inch away from him.

"This must be," he whispered as he removed her clothing. "You understand that I must have you."

Her only answer was a little nod of assent. If he didn't take her, she would shatter into a thousand pieces more cruel and cutting than glass.

Sharif eased her onto the bed. Holly lost all awareness of anything except the tip of his tongue, licking across her bare skin, finding inlets and arousing her to white heat.

Beneath them, the bed creaked, but in her mind they lay on thick blankets in a tent, far away in a misty land. For this night, she belonged to the sheikh and to his world.

Rising above her, he peeled off his clothes until his wildness was no longer hidden by the trappings of civilization. From his kneeling position, Sharif surveyed her as if she were his beloved possession.

Bracing himself over her, he brushed her lips with his. Holly arched upward, taking his mouth, teasing his male hardness with her core. Guiding him downward, offering herself, until he took her with one explosive thrust.

The suddenness of pleasure made her gasp. Colors shimmered through her in an ever-expanding circle as the sheikh claimed her again.

He murmured caressing phrases in a language she didn't understand, but she recognized its raw honesty and a joyous torment that matched her own.

Without warning, he stopped. Holding her and himself in balance.

"Sharif?" she whispered.

"Look at me."

His eyes were nearly black, and the shifting shad-

ows sculpted his face into sharp planes. He was both
the man she knew, and an alien warrior.

"I want you to know who is making love with
you," the sheikh said. "There must be no one else in
your mind but me."

"No one," she whispered. Who could compare to
him? Who could come close to this ardent conqueror?
Now she understood why she had never felt ready to
make love with Trevor. This was what she had been
waiting for. "Sharif…"

"No more words." His eyes half closed as he entered her again. At the same time, his roughened palm
caressed her velvety core just above their joining.

His hoarse cries matched hers as they reached ful-
fillment together. And floated in each other's arms
into a warm, dark cocoon of sleep.

WHEN HE AWOKE, Sharif took stock of his surroundings. Gray dawn light penetrated the blinds, and the
fire had shrunk to embers. Across the cabin, he could
hear Ben cooing, happily absorbed in his baby
thoughts.

Inside himself, he could tell that something essential had altered. His body felt purified and more in
harmony with his spirit.

Holly had given him a great gift last night. How
much had he changed?

Slowly, cherishing each detail, the sheikh allowed
himself to look at the woman beside him. He smiled
at the darkened tangle of hair across her cheek, and
the smooth creaminess of her bare skin.

Her lashes blinked open to reveal a sleep-befuddled
amber gaze. Leaning over, he kissed the tip of her
nose.

"Sharif?" She pulled the covers over her breasts, but not quickly enough to hide their smooth roundness. Temptation licked inside him. "Is it morning?"

"Yes, and the storm is over," he said.

She smiled impishly. "Are you speaking metaphorically?"

"Another storm of that nature is already looming on the horizon, I assure you," he said. "After so long, I fear we may be in for a siege of rough weather."

Holly's fingers feathered the hair along his temple. "Has it really been that long? Don't tell me the women in Alqedar don't scheme to get you in their beds."

"As for their scheming, I cannot say." An uncharacteristic laziness invaded Sharif, and he allowed himself to relax for a few moments longer. "But I have been with no one since my wife died."

"Nine years?" Her expression sobered. "You must have loved her with all your heart."

He never talked about Yona. Since the day she died, Sharif had held his grief tightly inside. Yet Holly was, after all, his lover.

"The problem is that I did not love her enough to put aside my selfishness," he said. "It is because of me that she died alone."

"What happened?" Holly asked.

"She died in childbirth," he said. "Along with our firstborn son."

She absorbed the information in stunned silence. "How awful," she said at last.

"Our rebel troops had just reclaimed Bahrim and were pressing on to the capital," Sharif said. "Yona had suffered complications but she refused to fly to Europe to a first-class hospital."

"She wanted to be near you," Holly said.

"I should have insisted that she go, but it seemed right to me that our child should be born in our own land," he said.

"I can understand that."

"Can you understand why I didn't stay in Bahrim with her?" he demanded. "When our troops continued on to the capital city of Jeddar, I wanted to share in the glory of the final battle."

"You're the leader of your people," she pointed out. "If you hadn't gone, they wouldn't have shared in the victory, either, would they?"

"I could have sent Zahad in my place," he said. "Instead, I left him to protect our palace. He sent word as soon as he saw how much blood Yona had lost, but by the time I arrived..." His eyes clouded. "I did not even have a chance to say good-bye."

Perhaps, he reflected, he would not feel so haunted if he had at least been present to hold Yona's hand. Sometimes at night he would awaken with a start, thinking she had cried out and that he must go to her before it was too late. But it had been too late for nine years.

"I didn't get to say goodbye to my sister, either," Holly said. "The day she left home, I'd been snappish with her. Maybe if I was more patient, she'd have confided in me. But we can't undo the past. We can only try to learn our lessons and not make the same mistakes again."

Sharif stroked her hair. "That is the problem. Last night, I was too caught up in my own desires to think about the future. About your future."

She rolled onto her side and supported her head on her hand. "I knew what I was doing."

Did she? "We used no protection," he said. "You could be carrying my child, Holly."

The corners of her mouth quirked upward. "I wouldn't mind."

"I suspect your fiancé would."

"Oh, Sharif." She lowered her head and pressed her cheek against his shoulder. "I can't think that far ahead. I can hardly think past the next five minutes. So how can I blame you?"

*Because I am a leader,* he wanted to say. *Others can afford to be lax. I have no right to such self-indulgence.*

And he *was* indulging himself, every hour that he spent away from Bahrim. Particularly now that its economic future had been threatened.

The subject reminded him of the reason for Holly's foray last night. "I do not mean to sound cold-hearted," he said, "but before you discovered your call was monitored, did you happen to get the name of a lawyer?"

"Edward Hoolihan," she said. "Trevor mentioned him right before I slammed down the phone and high-tailed it out of there."

Sitting up, Sharif ignored the rush of chill air. "Do you know this man?"

"Only by his reputation. But it's a good one. He's won some prominent cases."

Sharif weighed the possibilities. Should he contact the attorney now, or wait for Amy's arrival?

He scarcely noticed Holly's wistful expression as, lost in thought, he arose and went to dress for the day.

HOLLY HAD no intention of torturing herself with false hopes. She doubted she would conceive Sharif's baby from one encounter. And he'd certainly made no mention of her returning to Alqedar with him.

As far as she could tell, when he left America, that would be the last she ever saw of him. Well, they'd be lucky if they both survived that long, she reminded herself as she took her turn at dressing.

When she emerged from the bathroom, she heard Sharif talking on the phone in the front room. "That would be excellent, Mr. Hoolihan.... We will have to consider that.... I understand."

Not wanting to eavesdrop, Holly decided to check whether Alice had sent a message. Sure enough, when she logged onto the Internet, the screen flashed, You Have Mail.

> Hey, kid, the nurse came through with a home number for Manuel Estrellas. 555-4259.
> By the way, Trevor called last night and told me how he screwed up. Poor guy, he was just trying to rescue you. Maybe you should give him a break, huh?
> Come home soon.
> Love,
>
>                                        Alice

Holly scribbled down Manuel's number and sent a note of thanks. She considered e-mailing Trevor, too, but what would she say? That she forgave him, and hoped he would forgive her?

Trevor had been her friend and ally for so long, it was hard to imagine life without him. Yet what she felt for him was nothing like the deep and searing desire that Sharif aroused.

Soon, perhaps even today or tomorrow, she would see him in person. That would be time enough to face the issue of whether either of them still wanted to go ahead with their marriage.

No matter what might happen, she didn't regret last night. She would cherish the memory of holding Sharif as long as she lived.

Finished with his call, the sheikh came to talk to her. "Hoolihan is willing to take our case. However, he's pressing for Zahad and me to turn ourselves in."

"Does he understand that someone's trying to kill you?" she asked.

Sharif ran one hand through his hair. "He promises to communicate this fact to the police. I do not suppose they will believe us."

"Other people heard the gunshots in Placentia yesterday," Holly pointed out. "That's independent confirmation, right?"

"I will mention that to Mr. Hoolihan the next time I talk to him," he said. "He was on his way to court, so it won't be until this afternoon."

"Which gives us time to call Manuel." Holly showed him the number. "Will you help me interview him?"

"Of course." Leaning toward her, the sheikh took her hands in his. "Why should you think otherwise?"

"Because you've got so many other things to worry about," she said. "Like the problems in your country. But I keep seeing my sister lying there in the desert, and I think how scared and alone she must have been. I know we can't bring her back, but I want to find out who killed her. I want to give her that much."

She didn't bother to wipe the tears that ran down her cheeks. Sharif kissed them away.

"I will do everything I can," he murmured. "Jasmine was the mother of my son. Even if she were not, I would do this for you, Holly."

She wanted so much more from him. But it appeared that this would have to be enough.

ALTHOUGH THE storm was over, dark clouds gave the late afternoon sky an ominous cast. From the spot where he'd parked the pickup, Sharif could get only an angled view of Room 126 at the motel where Manuel had arranged to meet Holly.

"I will come inside with you," he said. "It is too dangerous to go alone."

She gripped the child seat as she planted a kiss on the baby's head. "The man's scared to death of you. Maybe he's just jumpy, or maybe he thinks you're the killer, but, from what he said, I'm sure he'll run if he sees you. Then we'll never find out what he knows."

According to Holly, Manuel had agreed to talk to her for Jazz's sake. He'd already been interviewed twice by the police, but, from their line of questioning, he wasn't convinced they were on the right track. Or else he had an agenda of his own.

The motel was one of perhaps a dozen clustered near Disneyland. Their crowded lots intersected those of fast-food restaurants, and small groups of tourists filled a nearby sidewalk. Amid the busy scene, the truck blended into the welter of parked vans and motor homes.

Sharif hated to let Holly out of his sight, especially

in the company of a man about whom they knew very little. But she was adamant, and time grew short.

"Remember that I'll be listening." He indicated the cloned phone that she held. "Go ahead. Dial me."

She nodded and obeyed. When his line buzzed, Sharif pressed start. "Can you hear me? Through the phone, I mean."

"Ouch. You don't have to talk so loud!" she said.

"Just as long as we're connected."

She tucked the phone inside the oversize knit jacket she'd borrowed from Sharif. They would keep the line open. He probably wouldn't be able to follow the conversation, with the phone hidden, but he could hear if she cried out.

Or if she uttered, loudly and clearly, the code phrase, "You don't really mean that." They'd chosen it to signal that something was seriously wrong.

Nevertheless, any number of things could go awry, he reflected. Once, Sharif had been too late to reach the woman he loved. No precaution could guarantee it wouldn't happen again.

INSIDE THE sparse motel room, Holly accepted Manuel's offer of the only seat, a hard, straight-backed chair. He was a pudgy man with black hair curling around his earnest face.

"You're darker than your sister," he said as she sat down.

"I dyed my hair." Distractedly, Holly twisted a dark-brown strand around her forefinger. "Anyway, thanks for talking to me."

"Somebody's gotta get at the truth. Maybe you can do it." He spoke above traffic noise that drifted through the open door.

"What exactly did you do at the clinic?" she asked.

"I started out as a medical technician," he said. "Mrs. Wheaton promoted me to what she called an administrative assistant. It's just a fancy name. She likes to promote workers from inside because she doesn't trust new people."

"Did you tell the police everything?" she asked.

"I tried, but they kept asking me what happened to Mrs. Wheaton, like I was responsible," he said. "And trying to trick me into telling them stuff about Jazz that the killer would know. They just want somebody to blame."

When a large truck rumbled by, the man closed the door. In the silence, Holly became aware of a faint noise coming over her cell phone. It was Ben, starting to fuss. "How well did you know my sister?" she asked quickly.

"I only saw her at the clinic. She was gorgeous." He picked up a can of soda and took a swig. "It was wrong that they lied to her. But Mrs. Wheaton, she did that sometimes."

As he spoke, the baby's complaints intensified. Manuel glanced irritably at the wall, as if he thought the sound came from the next room.

Knowing that Ben might be on the verge of a full-fledged crying spell, Holly considered trying to switch off her phone. Apparently the sheikh beat her to the punch, because the noise ended abruptly. He must have hung up, because the baby would never fall silent that fast.

She was on her own now. Sharif couldn't hear her unless she screamed, and maybe not even then.

''Did Mrs. Wheaton lie to all the surrogates?'' she asked.

''No, mostly to the parents. You know, the clients.'' Manuel switched the soda can back and forth between his hands. ''She would delete stuff out of the surrogates' files, like that they'd once used drugs. She said people were too fussy.''

Holly wished he would stop fidgeting. She felt nervous enough all by herself. ''Do you know how Jazz was recruited?''

''Somebody referred her, I think. Somebody that Mrs. Wheaton knew. But I don't know who.'' He started to take another drink, then set the can down and glanced toward the window.

''Are you afraid of someone?'' she asked.

''Maybe it's crazy but...'' His shoulders hunched. ''Mrs. Wheaton got real scared after Jazz ran away. Some phone calls that came in, I guess they musta been threats. That's when I decided to quit. I didn't want to be around when they figured out I was the one that told your sister the truth.''

''Any idea who it was?'' Holly pressed. ''Could it have been someone from the Middle East?''

''She got a few calls from that guy on the TV, what's his name? The sheikh's friend,'' he said.

''Zahad?''

''Yeah. But I don't know if he's the one that scared her.'' He tipped back the window shade and peered out.

Holly tried to concentrate on other possibilities, other details she might draw out of him. ''What about Dr. Lowrie? Could he have threatened Mrs. Wheaton?''

''He woulda talked to her in person, not on the

phone. Besides, he's a good guy. Hey, did you come here by yourself like I asked? I think I see somebody near my van.''

Holly couldn't tell him a point-blank lie. ''Sharif's in the pickup with the baby. Manuel, he didn't kill my sister.''

The shade dropped into place. ''You shoulda come alone! I swear, somebody's sneaking around. What's going on here?''

''It's okay.'' Holly spoke soothingly. ''We just want information.''

Manuel shifted back and forth on the balls of his feet, and then he lunged at her.

# Chapter Eleven

The sheikh muttered a few choice phrases at having to bring Ben along to a potentially hazardous situation—and at having to let Holly remain in that room alone.

He'd heard enough of the conversation to realize that the police considered Manuel a suspect. At the moment, it was hardly reassuring, even though it meant that at least the investigators weren't convinced of Sharif's guilt.

Along the parking lanes, vehicles came and went, and people continued to amble by, toting cameras and souvenir shopping bags. He caught snatches of German, Spanish and Asian tongues.

The baby squalled even louder. Sharif tried humming. Ben quieted briefly, then began grumbling again.

He'd been fed before they left the cabin, so hunger wasn't the problem, and it was too risky to change a diaper when they might need to drive off in a hurry. In desperation, Sharif turned on the radio.

Ben quieted as soon as he heard a country song. Apparently he liked music. Unfortunately, it further blocked the sheikh's chances of hearing any outcry from Holly. She was only a few dozen feet away, but inside that room, she might as well have been in Siberia.

On the radio, the music yielded to a staticky news bulletin. ''The body of missing…director Noreen Wheaton has…an abandoned warehouse…Los Angeles.''

Sharif turned up the volume.

''Mrs. Wheaton disappeared from her home in Harbor View late Monday or early Tuesday,'' the announcer said. ''Police have not indicated how she died or whether her death is connected to the murder of Hannah Jasmine Rivers.''

The reporter repeated what was previously known in the case, but gave no other new details.

Sharif smacked the steering wheel. Another woman was dead. And it might be, in some twisted way, because of him.

Until now, he'd harbored the faint hope that Jazz's tragedy wasn't connected to her surrogacy, but, as far as he knew, the two women were linked only by the pregnancy he had commissioned. It would be very strange indeed if the murders were unrelated.

There had to be some pattern that he ought to perceive, Sharif told himself. Perhaps one that involved the sniper attempts that had targeted him twice in the past few days.

He had considered Maimun's zealots the obvious suspects, but they would have little reason to go after the mother of his child, and even less to target the clinic director. A more likely perpetrator, he realized with a jolt, was the man sitting in the motel room right now, alone with Holly. A man who had known both Jasmine and Mrs. Wheaton.

Just then, the door to Room 126 slammed open. A

chunky, black-haired man hurried out, scowling, and half ran in the other direction.

Where was Holly? What had the man done to her?

Nothing else mattered, not the possibility that Sharif might get arrested or even that he might be shot by some unobserved sniper. He had to make sure Holly was all right.

He switched on the truck, backed out and drove toward the building. Further along the motel wing, he saw Manuel climb into a van.

Still no one else came out of Room 126.

Sharif was about to cross a driving lane when a couple of motorcycles sped around the corner and zoomed in front of him. He hit the brakes to avoid a collision.

As their roar faded, his ears caught the whirr of an ignition system not quite catching. It came from the direction of Manuel's van.

A warning flashed in his mind, something he'd learned during his military training. *Someone might have tampered with it.*

Sharif put the truck into park and threw himself over the baby.

From the van erupted a wall of noise and a sheet of flame. Glass and metal flew through the air.

People screamed and, nearby, a couple of vehicles collided. When Sharif dared to look again, the van had withered to a blackened heap with flames licking from its hood.

The truck had suffered no major damage, but then this blast hadn't been aimed at him. The target must have been Manuel.

First Jasmine. Then Noreen, and now Manuel. What kind of secrets had that clinic been hiding?

It crossed his mind that one of the motorcyclists might have thrown a grenade, but Sharif placed more credence on the missed ignition. The car had been wired with a bomb, and it had been done in a public place without being detected. This was the work of a professional.

As he pulled to the curb in front of the motel room, its newly scarred door started to open. At the same time, a blur of movement drew his gaze.

A dark figure, its face hidden by a ski mask, raced forward just as Holly came out of the room. Before Sharif could shout a warning, the masked man yanked her from her feet and threw her over his shoulder.

She tried to struggle, but must have had the wind knocked out of her. Amid the chaos, no one else was paying any attention.

Sharif leaped out of the truck. "Put her down!"

The shrill of approaching sirens made the assailant flinch. As the sheikh grabbed for Holly, the man swiveled indecisively and then, with a curse, flung her toward him.

The impact sent him staggering. In that split second, the attacker fled.

The sirens grew louder. Releasing a sharp breath of frustration, the sheikh surrendered the idea of giving chase. "Can you walk?"

"I—I'll try."

It was a good thing he took hold of Holly's arm, because at the first step, her knees gave way. He was helping her regain her balance when a paramedic unit halted in front of them.

"Are you hurt?" called a medic.

"Just shook up," Sharif said. Holly nodded in agreement. How much strength it took to hide her agitation, he could only guess. He'd seen trained soldiers go into shock after such a brush with danger.

"Well, take it easy," the man said as his partner drove on toward Ground Zero of the blast. Another paramedic unit and a fire truck had already arrived, and two police cars were pulling into the lot.

"What happened?" Holly asked, trembling. "I heard a blast."

"Someone blew up Manuel's van, with him inside. Let's get out of here. We can talk later." Sharif steered her to the truck.

As he boosted Holly inside, she gave the baby a quavery greeting, then sank back. The sheikh was grateful for her silence. He needed all his wits to get out of here before the cops cordoned off the area.

There was no sign of the man in the ski mask. He would have removed it by now, of course. Sharif studied the drivers of the vehicles they passed, but none of them looked familiar.

Before entering the motel lot earlier, he had circled it to assess escape routes. Now he knew enough to avoid the two main exits, which the police were already blocking, and veer into an alley.

A few seconds later, they emerged beside a hamburger stand, and the truck merged into a line of departing cars. Soon they were on the boulevard, heading away from the blast scene.

"Tell me what happened," Holly said, clasping her hands tightly together.

"Manuel came barreling out of the motel room. When he turned on his van, it went off like a firecracker," Sharif said. "I was afraid he might have hurt you."

"No. He saw someone fiddling with the van and I

guess he freaked when I admitted I'd brought you along.'' She took a couple of deep breaths. ''He jumped at me, like he was trying to scare me, and then he fled.''

''What took you so long getting out?'' Quite a bit of time had passed between Manuel's departure and hers.

She touched the baby's cheek as if his presence soothed her. ''I decided to take a look around, in case he'd left anything in the room. I guess that saved my life, huh? The whole room shook with the blast.''

If the bomb hadn't killed her, the assailant might have. She had come very close to dying, Sharif thought.

There was something else he had to consider. Holly had probably left fingerprints all over Room 126, which Manuel had rented, most likely in his own name. Once the police identified her, the paramedic would recall seeing the two of them outside.

Sharif's presence would again make him a suspect, and now the police would have reason to believe Holly was aiding and abetting his crimes. Even a kidnap victim wasn't immune to prosecution for joining her captors, he recalled from reading about the Patty Hearst case.

Holly needed to go home and resolve matters before she ended up either dead or in prison because of him.

HOLLY COULD move her limbs and even speak, but she felt disembodied, as if she were operated by remote control. That man in the ski mask, where had he come from? What had he meant to do with her?

She trembled as she relived the impact of being

seized from one side and jerked off her feet. The whole time, she'd been thinking that this was too bizarre to be real, that she ought to be able to take control. Yet she'd been helpless.

She hadn't even observed anything that could identify the man. He hadn't spoken. There'd been nothing distinctive about his clothing, and the only scent she recalled was the burning chemical fumes from the explosion.

As the sheikh drove, a newscast recounted the discovery of Noreen Wheaton's body. Had she, too, been snatched by surprise? Holly wondered.

She knew she ought to tear her thoughts away, but she couldn't. The man who'd grabbed her was still dominating her mind, and she resented him for that almost as much as for the incident itself.

At last her musings veered to another subject, but it was hardly more pleasant. Manuel. As she and Sharif fled, she'd glimpsed the smoldering van. Just a few minutes before, he'd been talking to her, and now he was dead.

Why? He'd already told the police what he knew. Could the killer have feared he'd held something back and revealed it to Holly?

How had the man found them, anyway? Had he been tailing Manuel?

The best thing to do, Holly decided was to review the few facts she'd gained at the motel. Perhaps Sharif could make more sense of them than she had.

"Manuel said that Mrs. Wheaton often removed negative information from the surrogates' files," she told him. "Things like previous drug use."

"So lying to your sister must have come easily to

her." The sheikh kept his eyes on the canyon road, which was littered with debris from the storm.

"He—he also thought Jazz was recruited by some-one Mrs. Wheaton knew." That wasn't very helpful, either, since Holly had no idea what circles the woman moved in. But maybe Dr. Lowrie's nurse did. "We could ask Alice to find out…"

"No." He veered around a large fallen branch. "She put us in touch with Manuel, and now he's dead. She won't have anything more to do with us. I wouldn't blame her if she tells the police everything she knows."

Of course she would, Holly acknowledged. Yet the loss of her one reliable contact was wrenching.

Until this moment, the normal world had seemed so close, as if she could easily move back into it. Now the ties were snapping, isolating them. "Sharif, I'm scared."

"I'm going to get you out of this mess." He sounded grim. "I dragged you into this, and it's long past time I let you go."

She didn't want to leave him, in spite of everything. "I'm the one who chose to jump into your car, and I've helped you of my own free will," she said. "I'm staying."

They drove along the canyon in silence. It wasn't until they pulled into the clearing in front of the cabin that he said, "I don't have a plan yet for sending you home, but I won't put you in harm's way again. This investigation is at an end."

Holly could see from his expression that he was in no mood to argue. Neither was she. After all, who could guess what might happen an hour or a day from now?

For most of her life, she had created hopeful visions of the future for herself, so clear they seemed inevitable. Since the first moment she felt a tug of attraction toward Sharif, however, she had been unable to imagine a future for the two of them, and yet it didn't matter.

Now she cherished, not images of what would be, but snapshots of these moments together. She memorized his gentle grip as he helped her to the ground, and the tenderness in his face as he lifted Ben from the child seat.

The sheikh had said he had no definite plan for sending her away. Until he did, Holly would live in the present, fully and completely.

SHARIF DIDN'T intend for them to make love again. He knew that Holly needed time to recover from the shock of the afternoon, and he had many arrangements to make. Above all, he didn't want them to draw any closer.

After dinner, when the baby was sleeping in the basket, he busied himself searching the Internet while Holly bathed. He had expected her to go right to bed afterward, but when he looked up again, it was to see her standing before him with only a towel wrapped around her curves.

"Maybe I have to lose you," she said, "but I haven't lost you yet."

"You have been through too much today," he protested raggedly, fighting his impulse to touch her.

"Then help me forget." Drawing him to his feet, she let the towel drop.

Desire hardened inside Sharif. He wanted her at

every level, this woman who had taught him how to love again after so many years.

He loved the smooth hair that tangled in his hands, the hair that she had dyed for his sake. He relished the teasing curve of her mouth, and the little hesitations that reminded him of her vulnerability.

He let her arouse him with her mouth and hands as she guided him to the bed. He felt like a savage creature, transfixed.

But the wildness would not be stayed for long. As Holly drew him down, it burst through his restraint.

Almost roughly, Sharif ran his hands along her breasts and caught her hips. He kissed her forehead, his mouth tracing the straight nose down to the warm mouth.

When he claimed her, her moans and eager movements drove him onward into a blaze of pure bliss. After nine years of sorrow, he had found joy again.

In the dream, Sharif raced through the palace in Alqedar's capital city. Separated from the other rebels, he was searching, endlessly searching, for someone.

The evil leader, Maimun. The man who had killed his father.

Sharif was instinctively reaching for his Uzi when he awoke. The image of the palace hallways remained as vivid in his mind, however, as if he were reliving that day.

He could almost hear the shouting and machine gunfire. Nor would he ever forget what had happened next.

Stepping into a luxurious room hung with tapestries, he had lifted his gun to spray anyone who might be hiding. Then, from an alcove, he heard the frightened whimper of a child.

Alarmed that he had come so close to killing an innocent, he'd crossed the room and pulled back the curtain. But there was no child there. Maimun himself, having fled his troops like the coward he was, leaped out with a knife and slashed Sharif across the ribs.

There was no time even to reach for the gun. Scarcely feeling the pain from his wound, he had grasped Maimun's wrist and strained, inch by inch, to turn the blade until he drove it into the tyrant's chest.

Sharif's hands clenched at the memory. He had later learned that on that same day, in another palace halfway across the country, Yona had bled to death, the baby dying in her womb. That day he had saved himself, but lost those most precious to him.

In the darkness, it took a while for his emotions to calm. Gradually, he became aware of Holly's regular breathing and the way the air hummed with her nearness.

He could no longer deny that he loved her. He also did not doubt that the old dream must have come to him for a reason.

It was a warning, that this time he must not fail to protect the woman he loved. And he could see only one way to do that.

He must find a way to return her to her own world, this very day.

OVER BREAKFAST on Thursday, Holly watched as yesterday's bombing scene appeared on a national news broadcast. In her confusion yesterday, she hadn't realized how much the parking lot resembled a war zone.

Mercifully, no one but Manuel had died, and the other injuries were limited to cuts and bruises. However, the announcer pointed out, this latest development in an ongoing case had for the first time threatened bystanders. The murders and abductions had become matters of widespread public concern.

Yet there was no report of the man in the mask, Holly realized. Apparently no one but she and Sharif had encountered him.

The sheikh finished clearing the dishes, set his laptop in front of her and attached his cell phone to the modem. "It is time to check your e-mail."

"But Alice wouldn't message me now!"

"The police might," he said. "She has probably given them your address. They might offer a way for you to leave."

"They're wasting their time." She stared up at him defiantly.

"Did I tell you I have heard from Amy?"

The news deflated her. Holly wasn't ready for things to change, even though she knew they must. "Is that who you were talking to a while ago? I thought it was Zahad."

"She's arriving in Los Angeles this morning," he said. "She was not happy that I have arranged for an attorney on my own, but she accepts my decision. I wish for her to take Ben home as quickly as possible."

His face had a drawn look this morning, as if he hadn't slept well. What chilled Holly was the opaque steeliness of his voice. She had hoped last night would bring them closer, but instead he had withdrawn from her.

"Someone needs to explain to her about him," she said. "What he likes, how he prefers to be held. Besides, I want to meet her and make sure—"

"She has two children of her own." He spoke crisply. "Check your mail, Holly."

There was nothing to be gained by arguing the point. Reluctantly, she typed in the commands.

There was one message. It came from Trevor.

"Alice says you swear this sheikh won't hurt you," he wrote. "Honey, the only thing I know is that you're in a lot of danger. I don't want to lose you the way we lost Jazz.

"I've arranged to be at Edward Hoolihan's law office this afternoon at two o'clock. It's as close to a neutral place as I could think of. You can come alone, or those men can come too if they want to consult with him. No one will notify the police. Attorney-client privilege, remember?

"Please come back. I want to marry you more than ever. No matter what you've been through, remember that I've known you all your life. Nobody loves you more than I do."

Holly's tears blurred her view. Instead of the screen, she saw Trevor's familiar face with the square jawline, the self-deprecating grin.

Behind her, Sharif finished reading the message. "You chose a good man," he said.

"I'm not choosing him."

"You chose him once," the sheikh reminded her. "Now you must go back."

"No!"

His hand on her shoulder prevented her from rising.

"Listen to me, Holly. Do you honestly think we could have a life together? What happened between us was an accident. It was not meant to be."

"You're wrong!" She ducked out of his grasp and rose to confront him. "Last night—"

Sharif drew himself up. He seemed taller, this morning, and infinitely more remote. "I admit that I feel a strong attraction to you. You are a beautiful woman, and after nine years alone, who could resist?"

She brushed his statement aside. "It isn't just physical and you know it."

"It's true that I admire you." He spoke smoothly. "You are very brave. Yona would have liked you. But you don't belong in my country, Holly, and I don't belong in yours. Nothing can change that."

A lump formed in her throat. "We're not living in the nineteenth century. We can find a way."

He shrugged. "I promised to try to solve your sister's death, but I have failed. Once Amy takes the baby, Zahad and I will slip away."

"I'll join you." She hadn't planned to say that. She hadn't thought that far ahead.

A muscle jumped in the sheikh's jaw. "I am not asking you to join me. Do you fail to understand me, Holly? Please don't force me to be cruel."

Her body tightened into a knot of pain. "You don't want me to come? What we've shared doesn't mean anything to you?"

"Please don't spoil what we've had with recriminations," he said quietly. "We are very different, Holly. For me, an experience can be perfect in itself. That doesn't mean I need or want for it to continue once it becomes inconvenient."

Inconvenient? Is that how he saw their relationship?

The indifference in his words chilled her. But what broke Holly's heart was the look in his eyes.

It was pity.

## Chapter Twelve

A rushing in Holly's ears nearly drowned out Sharif's next words. He was saying that he believed she would be safer away from him.

"Once you surface, you won't have to hide from the police anymore," he said. "No more getting shot at, either."

"If I'm not a target, then why did that man grab me yesterday?" she demanded.

"Because you met with Manuel," he said. "This whole investigation was a mistake. We did nothing but expose ourselves, and others, to harm."

He turned away as he spoke. For that, Holly felt grateful. At some level, she believed, she had touched his heart, but how could she be sure?

She was losing not only the child she loved, but the man as well. Bittersweet memories of these past few days would stay with her always. Yet she knew she couldn't keep him.

Pride gave Holly the strength to do what needed to be done. To put aside her feelings, as Sharif had, and plan for the inevitable.

"I want to be the one to hand over the baby to your cousin," she said. "Amy's going to raise my only nephew. Surely you won't deny me the chance to meet her.''

He glanced at her sharply. "Only if we can arrange a rendezvous before two o'clock."

"I understand," she said. "Do you think Amy would want to meet us at the lawyer's office?"

"I will solicit Zahad's opinion. In any case, I need to fill him in on the situation." He sat at the table and opened his laptop computer.

"Whatever you think best." Biting her lip, Holly went to take the baby from his basket. She needed to get him ready for their last outing together.

THE MATTER had gone well, Sharif told himself. Holly had accepted his claim that he could end their relationship without a backward glance. She had not even yielded to tears.

Their closeness had sensitized him, however, to such small clues as the way her lips quivered and she avoided his glance. He wished he could take this sadness from her and make it his own, to spare her. But he was doing the best he could.

When he e-mailed Zahad about Trevor's offer and the plan to return Holly, his cousin responded quickly. "Do not let Amy meet you at the lawyer's office! If it is a trap, she and your son will be caught in it."

He was right, Sharif conceded. Although he didn't believe Trevor had arranged the meeting as a ploy, the man might go back on his word and alert the police. That created the possibility that someone could get trigger-happy.

"We will meet Amy somewhere else," he wrote. "Before two o'clock, please observe Hoolihan's building for signs of a stakeout. And make sure the coast stays clear.''

''Of course,'' his cousin messaged. ''However, I find it hard to believe that Holly can be trusted to give up the child.''

The sheikh's gaze traveled to the chair where she sat cradling Ben. Her dark hair cocooned the two of them, and he heard her voice catch as she sang softly.

Of course it would be difficult, but he knew how strong she was. ''I have complete faith in her,'' he wrote.

Zahad didn't pursue the subject. Instead, he replied, ''If you wish, the two of us can leave the country tonight. I will make the arrangements.''

Should they not turn themselves in, as the attorney had urged? Sharif wondered. But events in Alqedar demanded their immediate attention.

''Very well. I leave it in your hands,'' he wrote, and signed off.

No doubt he and Zahad would run into some danger during their escape, whether in the hold of a fishing vessel or in the back of a small plane, but he owed it to his people. Legal matters with the U.S. authorities could be sorted out later.

Holly busied herself dressing Ben while he explained that he didn't want Amy to meet them at Hoolihan's office. In the morning light, her translucent skin gave her a fragile air, but she listened with quiet determination.

''I know where we should go, then,'' she said when he finished. ''To a mall. The more public, the better.''

''This killer thinks nothing of risking the lives of bystanders,'' he pointed out. ''We saw that yesterday.''

She wiggled the little boy's arms into long sleeves. "He'd have to find us first. We won't be sitting in one place, the way Manuel's van was."

On short notice, he could think of no better alternative. "Which mall would you suggest?"

While she tugged overalls onto the baby, Holly described the main entrance to a mall that was only a few miles from the attorney's building. Worriedly, she added, "Do you think this man might pick up Amy's trail?"

"I am sure my cousin has taken the precaution of making several reservations, probably at more than one airport," he said.

"She sounds like quite a woman," Holly said. "I wish I could have the chance to know her better."

They would like each other, he thought. In fact, with her quick mind and strong nerve, Holly would be a great asset to Bahrim.

If only someday he might return to claim her, after the killer was found and his own name cleared. But, Sharif reminded himself, events would not stand still.

Three days ago, he had torn Holly from her wedding and thrust her into a maelstrom. In her confusion, it was no wonder she had become vulnerable to him.

Once she was restored to the man who had first claim on her, she would gradually recover. Soon the events of this week would seem like a bad dream. It would be the ultimate act of selfishness to disrupt her life a second time.

Ruthlessly, Sharif crushed the last spurt of hope. He must say goodbye to this woman and never look back.

AS THEY CRUISED a parking lane near the mall entrance, Holly realized that subconsciously she had been expecting to see a woman in traditional Arabic dress and headscarf. From Sharif's comments, however, she suspected Amy knew how to blend into an American crowd.

"What exactly does your cousin look like?" she asked.

"A bit shorter than you." He stopped to let a sedan back out of a space. "She wears her black hair at chin length. Sometimes she bleaches a few strands for the effect."

"How does she dress?" It was easier to keep talking than to think about the baby between them, his little eyes bright as he gazed from one to the other. He was so dear and so loving, it hurt to realize that he would grow up among strangers.

*He isn't yours. He belongs with his father.* Holly repeated the words to herself, over and over.

"When she travels, Amy wears business suits." As they resumed their snail's pace along the lane, he indicated a group of shoppers dressed in typically casual jeans and sweaters. "Around here, we should have no trouble spotting her."

It was a few minutes past one, by the truck's clock. Amy had assured Sharif that she would take a cab directly from the airport, where she'd been due to arrive just after eleven.

The flight, according to recorded information, had arrived on time. Even the weather was cooperating, with sunshine breaking intermittently through the clouds. And at this time of day, the freeways wouldn't be crowded.

So where was she? Holly surveyed the arched entranceway.

On a bench perched three teenage girls, chattering happily. Two women passed them, pushing baby carriages.

The pickup idled down another row of parked cars. So far, Holly hadn't seen any security vehicles.

If Sharif was worried about his cousin, he hid it well. "She might have had trouble finding a cab," he said. "Split-second timing hardly ever works in real life."

"Maybe she decided to do a little shopping," Holly joked, although she didn't feel very humorous.

"She certainly wouldn't be alone. There are a lot of people at this mall, for a weekday," Sharif said. She expected to hear some comment about how this fact aided or hindered their plan. Instead, he added, "Perhaps we should build one in Alqedar."

"A mall?" she asked. "Why?"

"Our wealthy residents spend their money abroad," he said. "A mall was proposed for our capital city, Jeddar, but the small merchants protested that they would be driven out of business."

"The big anchor stores draw the customers," she pointed out, "but there are small shops and booths inside the mall."

"It would be worth studying." Their path brought them past the entrance again. Still no Amy. "Is this a typical mall?"

Holly was so accustomed to thinking of the sheikh as a soldier that she'd almost forgotten his involvement in his land's economic growth. "Yes, I guess so. Except for the discount megamalls."

"What are those?"

"They're located further away from urban centers,

but people don't seem to mind driving to get a bargain,'' she said.

A ray of sunlight teased his brown hair and softened his strong features. ''This might interest President Dourad. It could create opportunities for some of the poorest areas of Alqedar.''

It was nearly 1:15. Holly had had more than enough chitchat. ''How long should we stick around?''

''Let's cruise the rest of the mall.'' The truck went straight instead of curving on its circuit. ''Perhaps she is waiting at the wrong place.''

Holly felt her hands growing damp. What if something had happened to Amy?

''There she is!'' Relief rang in Sharif's voice.

They had left the entrance area and were approaching one of the department stores. Instead of being tucked into a sheltered junction of two mall wings, the store thrust out into a side lot.

A woman with frosted black hair waited at the sidewalk's edge. Of medium height, she had lively, dark eyes and wore a long-skirted wool suit.

Spotting them, she waved. They pulled into a nearby parking space.

''Stay here.'' Sharif swung out and checked in all directions, while his cousin made an impatient face and marched toward them.

''What did you do, go out for ice cream? I've been here fifteen minutes!'' she called as she approached. ''Give me a hug, you renegade. Isn't that what the press is calling you? Or worse!''

He chuckled. ''It's good to see you, Amy.''

Standing on tiptoe in her stylish half boots, the small woman hugged Sharif. ''And where is my nephew? I am amazed he has survived your tender loving care.''

He gave Holly an all-clear sign. Her hands were so stiff, however, that it took several tries to undo the straps holding Ben in his seat, and her fingers slipped on the door lock before she got it open.

"So, you are the aunt!" Amy came to Holly's door. "How have you put up with this big lug all this time?"

"It...hasn't been easy." She tried to match the woman's light tone.

"Let me hold this little darling. Do you mind?" From her tote bag, Amy retrieved a cloth baby carrier and strapped it around her shoulders. "Oh, he is so darling! I would like to have another baby but Harry says no, we must devote our efforts to building up Bahrim. Maybe the old days when women stayed home weren't so bad, eh?" She didn't sound as if she meant it, though.

Holly couldn't help liking her. Carefully, she transferred the baby into Amy's grasp.

The woman murmured what sounded like endearments in a foreign language. Babbling happily, Ben plucked at her jacket.

"I know it is hard to trust a stranger," she told Holly as she slid him into the carrier, which fit over her chest. "Believe me, he is very precious to us. He will never want for anything. Especially love."

In spite of the kind words, a void opened inside Holly. Soon this baby would lose all memory of his previous life, but she would never forget even the tiniest detail about him.

"Where is your cab?" Sharif came around the

truck to join his cousin. "Did you ask the driver to wait?"

"Yes, at another entrance," she said. "It would be too conspicuous here."

He nodded. "We can drive you around. It will be a squeeze, but—"

"Sharif, look." Amy stared past him.

Holly turned to see a sedan with dark windows hurtling toward them along the perimeter roadway. "Get down!" Sharif snapped.

Holly ducked into the pickup's cab. A second later, a shot whined past the door.

Keeping low, the sheikh half rolled and half climbed into the driver's seat. More shots rang out.

"Where are Amy and Ben?" Holly gasped.

"They vanished into a row of cars," he said. "We must draw the gunmen off so they can reach the mall."

She grabbed the armrest as the truck spun backward and careened down the aisle in reverse. At any moment, she expected another spray of bullets.

Tires screeched, and Holly was thrown to one side despite her seat belt. Her chest aching, she clung to the armrest as they twisted through the lot. At least she didn't hear any more firing. The gunman must have been busy driving, or else couldn't get his aim.

A stolen glance through the windshield showed a station wagon backing heedlessly out of its space. "Watch out!" Sharif cried as they cleared the vehicle by inches.

Their pursuer wasn't so lucky. A moment later, metal crunched, and then an engine revved furiously as the sedan driver tried to get away.

The truck jounced onward. "Is he coming?" Holly asked.

"Their bumpers are hooked," Sharif said. "He is bailing out. Running."

"What about Amy? We have to go back and find her."

"She'll cut through the mall to her cab," he said. "He's not even trying to head in that direction. She's safe, Holly."

She had a hard time not insisting that they search for Ben. But they might only make things worse. "What about the gunman? There's only one? Who is it?"

"I cannot tell," he said. "And I will not endanger you by swinging back. It won't take him long to steal a car, or commandeer one. We need to hurry before the police—"

He broke off to stare in disbelief at something ahead. It was a motorcycle, scooting out of the mall onto the adjacent street.

There was no mistaking Zahad's muscular figure bent over the handlebars. Or, clinging behind him, Amy's smaller shape in the wool suit, still carrying the baby on her front.

Were they out of their minds, risking Ben's life on a motorcycle? What was Zahad doing here anyway? She'd heard Sharif on the phone tell him to stake out Hoolihan's building.

"Did you know…?" she began.

"I didn't even tell him where we were meeting." The truck roared forward, giving chase.

"You mean…he and Amy and the gunman…?" Her breath came short.

"Like a fool, I never saw it coming!" They ran a

red light at the mall exit and tore after the bike. "We have to get Ben back. That must have been their plan all along, to steal my son."

The cycle darted between cars, gaining momentum until it vanished in heavy traffic. Sharif's attempts to change lanes got him nowhere. They were stuck in a jam.

Just when Holly didn't think matters could get worse, a police car flashed them over. He must have seen them run the light. The policeman might not suspect their identities yet, but they were too notorious for him to miss the connection once he got a good look at them.

Sharif's jaw worked. She guessed he was debating whether to attempt an escape, but after a few agonizing seconds, he moved to the curb.

The cruiser halted behind them. Instead of getting out, however, the officer sat talking on his radio. In the side mirror, Holly saw him shrug, make a gesture of dismissal toward them, and set his car into motion. As he went by, his siren nearly deafened her.

"He must have been called out on something big," Holly guessed. "Maybe the gunfire at the mall."

Sharif shifted back into traffic. He wore a distant expression as if he, too, were stunned by the events of the past few minutes.

"Where do you think they'll take Ben?" Holly discovered that her hands were shaking.

"I have no idea," he admitted. "Zahad's been running rings around me this whole time. He and Amy must have planned for her to wait in the wrong place to throw us off guard."

"Maybe it isn't what it appears." Holly clung to the slim hope that she hadn't really handed Ben to someone who intended to harm him. "Why would their accomplice have shot at us on Monday when Zahad was driving?"

"To throw me off the track," he said. "If so, it worked."

Holly's mind kept coughing up details about Zahad. She pictured him bringing their supplies and the guns to the cabin. He could have killed them both, while they were unarmed.

Maybe there'd been a strategic reason to delay. To cast the blame, perhaps, onto some unidentified zealot, so Zahad's reputation in Bahrim wouldn't be stained with blood.

In any case, nothing could erase the image of him and Amy fleeing with Ben tucked between them. It seared Holly's memory.

"Why would they do this?" she asked as they drove.

"No one is immune to ambition." Beside her, Sharif had become an ice sculpture.

"They want power in Bahrim?" she asked. "You said they're from different sides of your family."

"And they've had a sort of rivalry. It never occurred to me..." He swallowed. "They must have decided to throw in their lots together. Amy has certainly found a way to thrust her husband onto center stage."

"What about Zahad?"

"He is the elder son of a sheikh, so he should have become head of his tribe in time, but his father has named his younger half brother as heir."

"So he got cheated," Holly said.

Sharif's eyes narrowed. "Not by me. I do not care

about power or about wealth. Only the well-being of our people, and about my son.''

"I can't believe I just handed him to her." Holly hugged herself. "We have to get Ben back before they can hurt him."

"*I* have to get him back," the sheikh said. "And I will."

When the truck slowed, she realized they had reached Edward Hoolihan's law office. "I can't leave now."

"You must." He leaned across her to open the door. When his body brushed hers, she felt the tension welling inside him. "Get out!"

"You need me. A lookout who knows the area." She fought to win him over with logic.

"I can fight better alone," he growled. "I should have depended less on others all along. Besides, you need to tell the police that Ben has been abducted. "

"They'll ask where we were hiding—"

"Tell them everything," he said.

The longer they sat here arguing, the greater the chance of someone catching them. And today even Holly couldn't bend Sharif's iron will.

"All right." *Except that we're lovers. Except that there's a connection between us that nothing can erase.* She rested one foot on the running board. "But when this is over—"

"It is over now," he said. "As far as you are concerned. Marry this man Trevor. Let him protect you. He can do it better than I."

His cavalier dismissal infuriated her. "Sharif, please! Don't—"

"From this point on, there is nothing between us."

Sharif's eyes met hers without a flicker of emotion. "If you refuse to accept it, that is your folly."

Holly wanted to pound him with her fists. And to hold him so tightly that he could never escape. The only tool she had was words, so she used them. "I can't make you care about me. But I love you, and nothing is going to change that."

She jumped to the sidewalk and ran into the building.

# Chapter Thirteen

Sharif had to clear his mind, to think, to plan, before he erupted like a volcano.

He couldn't allow himself to dwell on the fact that he had just ordered the woman he loved to marry someone else. At least she would be safe. There would no longer be any reason for his cousins to harm her.

As he drove away, he reminded himself that blind trust had nearly destroyed him. Now he must examine this betrayal and make sense of it.

Who had been the instigator, Zahad or Amy? Or had it been the seemingly mild-mannered Harry?

Even now, Sharif could hardly credit the evidence of his own senses. He knew these three people almost as well as he knew himself, or so he'd believed. How could they be traitors? And where were they taking Ben?

Surely someone at home had heard rumors, or at least snatches of conversation, that could help his understanding. Perhaps they could even put him on Zahad's trail.

The person who came to mind was his aunt Selima. She was, of course, Amy's aunt as well as his. But having seen one of her brothers die at the hands of a tyrant, and having lived through the repressive reign of Maimun, she surely would have no stomach for sedition.

He pulled into a medical center parking lot to make a call, but before he could dial, his mobile phone rang. He hoped it was not Holly, that nothing had gone wrong for her. ''Yes?'' he demanded.

The voice on the other end shocked him past speaking. ''I know how this must look,'' Zahad said. ''It is not as it seems.''

Sharif remained silent.

''Amy called earlier and told me of your plan to meet at the mall,'' he said. ''I did not believe Holly would give up the baby. I thought perhaps she and that fiancé of hers would trick you, so I kept watch.''

''You told Amy to meet us at the wrong entrance?''

''Of course. If it were a trap, that would be vital.''

''It *was* a trap.'' Sharif heard the ice in his tone. He was beyond anger. ''No one knew of that meeting place except you, me, Amy and Holly. Yet the gunman was there.''

He heard his cousin's exasperated breath. ''Yes, I told you, I know how it looks! I don't know how he found us. Amy says that at the airport she had the feeling someone was watching her, but she thought she had eluded him.''

The story sounded so plausible, he almost believed it. Not quite. Not this time.

Then, in the background, he heard Ben cooing. Sharif couldn't abandon his son, no matter how strongly he suspected that another snare was being set.

''What do you want?'' he asked.

"I want what you want, cousin. We will give you the baby," Zahad said. "We will meet wherever you say. If you trust me enough, we can leave this country using the arrangements I have made. Or you can go your own way. I wish only to prove my loyalty to you, who are dearer to me than a brother." Ruefully, he added, "In my case, quite a bit dearer."

The ironic reference to his half brother was so typical of Zahad's dry humor that Sharif felt a leap of affection, and with it, a touch of self-doubt. His cousin had fought and worked at his side all their adult lives. Hadn't the man earned a second chance?

"All right, we will meet. At four-thirty." That gave him a little more than two hours to decide on a suitable location.

"Where?" asked his cousin.

Sharif remembered some signs he'd seen en route to the restaurant in Placentia, and they gave him an idea. He decided not to reveal very much of it yet, however. "Pull off the 57 freeway in the city of Fullerton. At a little past four, I will call and give you further details."

"Very well." Zahad didn't hesitate, which was a good sign. If the man planned a subterfuge, he might be reluctant to put himself at such a disadvantage.

On the other hand, who knew how many accomplices he had and could position rapidly? And of course he knew that any reluctance on his part would alienate Sharif.

It was difficult to play a strategy game with a man who could second-guess your every move, the sheikh reflected. In choosing a meeting site, it might be best to act on impulse so that no one, even himself, could predict what place he would select. He might even change his mind and not meet them at all.

After ending the call, he remembered his plan of phoning Selima. It still seemed like a good idea.

As a precaution, he moved the truck to another side of the medical building. No sense in arousing anyone's curiosity about why he was sitting here for so long.

Then he dialed his aunt's number.

HOLLY'S HAND was shaking so badly that it took several tries before she pinpointed Edward Hoolihan's name on the lobby's glass-covered list. His office was on the second floor.

The sound of gunshots echoed in her mind, overshadowing the carpeted whisper of her tennis shoes as she walked to the elevator. Faces flashed before her. Amy. Ben. Sharif. Even Zahad, although she retained only a general impression of the man.

What had they done to her baby? How could anyone hurt that little sweetheart?

The elevator doors opened. At an unexpected metallic scrape, Holly flinched.

The lift was empty. No bombs. No bullets. No assassins lurking in the corners.

Inside, she gripped the handrail to keep her knees from crumpling. Until now, Holly had been too preoccupied with fast-moving events for the shocks to sink in. Now they seemed to be ganging up on her.

When the doors opened on the upper floor, she gathered her strength, released the rail and stepped into the hall. She didn't want Trevor to see her this upset. He'd been through enough stress himself, these past few days.

She struggled to walk with a steady gait. Smiling might be beyond the realm of possibility, but at least she could push firmly on the door labeled "Edward Hoolihan, Attorney at Law" and stride inside.

From a couch in the waiting room, Trevor looked up. Relief washed across his face as he tossed a magazine aside and got to his feet. "Thank God!"

As his arms closed around her, Holly burst into tears. It was the last thing she'd meant to do.

She was distantly aware of other people fussing around them, and of murmured questions. Where was the baby? Were the sheikh and his aide coming?

"They're gone" was all she managed to say before a fresh bout of weeping shook her.

"Did they hurt you?" Trevor demanded, then immediately answered himself. "Obviously they did! We need to get you to a doctor."

"I'm—all—right." Her words might have been more convincing if her lips weren't shaking.

Another man mentioned trauma. Trevor rested his cheek against Holly's hair. "Kid, I'll hunt those creeps down if it's the last thing I do."

"N-no," she stammered. "It's n-not Sharif's fault."

From Trevor's soothing reply, she could tell that he believed she was too distressed to think straight. He stopped making threats against the sheikh, though.

"Ms. Rivers, I'm Edward Hoolihan," said the other man. Peeking up, she made out graying hair and a concerned expression. "I can't represent you because of conflict of interest, and neither can your fiancé. If you like, however, I can arrange for another attorney. You'll need representation when you talk to the police."

"Thanks, Ed," Trevor said. "Not just yet, though. Look at her. She's in no condition to be debriefed."

"It's okay," Holly said into his jacket. "I want to tell them…they need to know that…" She couldn't finish the sentence.

"You see what I mean?" Trevor told his colleague. "Hey, you don't have to tell me it's important to catch Jazz's killer. But I'm concerned about Holly's health, mental and physical. I wasn't kidding about seeing a doctor."

"You have a point," Hoolihan conceded. "Don't delay contacting the police too long, though."

"We won't." Trevor shook hands with the man. "Thanks for letting me wait at your office. The cops have a disconcerting habit of popping into mine."

Gently, he guided her out of the building. "Honey, who's your regular doctor?"

"I don't have one. I g-go to a clinic," she said. "Anyway, I—I'm not hurt, just—maybe I should eat." She and Sharif had been too busy to stop for lunch.

Trevor held the door of his Cadillac. Holly sank into the cushions with a guilty sense of luxury. Right now, distressed as she was, the physical comfort came as a relief.

"I've arranged for a big meal at my house." Trevor came around to the driver's seat. "To make up for the wedding feast we missed. Think you can wait till we get home?"

Without realizing it, Holly had been picturing herself returning to her apartment. But she'd given it up, the day of the wedding. Her fiancé naturally assumed that his house was now her home, too.

Well, she wasn't the Holly Rivers of three days

ago. Her marriage plans seemed very far away. How could she possibly be expected to fit into her old life after what she'd experienced?

"In case you didn't want to see a doctor, Alice sent something for you." From his pocket, Trevor retrieved a small lumpy envelope.

Inside were two yellow capsules. "What's this?"

"A mild sedative." From a built-in rack beneath his seat, he selected a bottle of mineral water. "She said they were left from last year, something about needing them after a quarrel with her son. It ought to relax you."

Holly didn't want her mind any more clouded than it already was. On the other hand, the delayed shock had hit hard. In her present condition, she knew she couldn't answer the police detectives' questions coherently. "How long before this stuff wears off?"

"A couple of hours, I think." Trevor unscrewed the top and handed her the bottle. "Then we can eat dinner and take our time. When you feel up to it, I'm sure the detectives will be happy to talk to you, no matter how late it is."

If Alice had found these pills mild, what harm could they do? Holly washed the capsules down with water. There, it was done.

The engine started. By the time they reached the street, she already felt calmer. Within a few minutes, a pleasantly dizzy sensation crept through her, and she knew she was falling asleep.

IT TOOK SEVERAL agonizing minutes to get Selima on the phone. Sharif had forgotten that, with the eleven-hour time difference, it was the middle of the night in Bahrim.

The first sound his aunt uttered was half yawn and half groan. When she heard his name, she said, ''Tell me you are on your way home with my great-nephew, and I will forgive you for waking me.''

''I wish that I could.'' He sketched the story of Amy's arrival and the fiasco at the mall.

''Oh, dear,'' Selima said. ''This cannot be as it seems. Not Zahad and Amy.''

''You have heard no rumors about them?'' Sharif asked. ''No gossip about a plot?'' His aunt always kept her ear to the ground.

''Nothing,'' she said. ''By the way, President Dourad is trying to get hold of you. He left his private number. I didn't give him yours because you said never to give it to anyone. I did try to reach you but your line was always busy. Did I do the right thing?''

''Yes, of course.'' It had never occurred to Sharif that the president of Alqedar might want to call him in America. Was this about nationalizing the Jubah cloth industry?

Tensely, he copied the number and thanked his aunt. Her closing words were ''Amy and Zahad would not dare harm that baby. If they do, I will personally strangle them.''

He dialed the president's number but didn't activate it, then put the truck into gear and headed for the freeway. Not until he had blended into the light midafternoon traffic did he push Send.

And hoped the leader of his country wouldn't mind being disturbed at this hour.

HOLLY DRIFTED in and out of consciousness, lulled by the velvety motion of the Cadillac and the drug in her bloodstream. At last she sank into a dream in which she sat across a conference table from two police detectives.

She tried to tell them that Ben was in danger, but they twisted everything she said to implicate Sharif. Finally she blurted that if he was guilty, they would have to blame her, too.

The men gave her a confession to sign. She knew she must not, but she had no lawyer and she was so tired. Finally, struggling as if through a thick liquid, she put her name to the document.

And tried to wake up. But she was much, much too sleepy.


SHEIKH ABDUL Dourad took the call at once. "I could not sleep, anyway," he said. "I had hoped you would contact me, old friend. There are important developments."

A Highway Patrol car entered the freeway just ahead. Sharif eased his pressure on the accelerator. "What has happened?"

"Yesterday, my intelligence agency captured a former follower of Maimun's," he said. "He was working as a steward on Air Alqedar."

That was the airline that Sharif and Zahad had flown to America. Amy had probably taken it as well.

"So they have followed our trail close at hand." The CHP cruiser got sandwiched between a couple of slow-moving cars. The truck would either have to come abreast of it or make an obvious nuisance of itself by driving too slowly in the faster-moving lane.

"When he learned that he will be charged with murder if anyone dies as a result of his spying, he was most willing to talk to us," the president continued. "He has been feeding information to Maimun's brother, Yusuf Gozen, who has sworn vengeance on you.''

The fact that Sharif had slain the dictator in self-defense made no difference, he knew. Maimun's brother was a zealot who cared nothing for such details.

The man had nothing in common with Zahad and Amy, except, possibly, a desire to get rid of Sharif. Still, such an alliance was not impossible.

''Do you know if Yusuf is conspiring with anyone from Bahrim?'' Sharif asked.

''I have heard no mention of it. Why?''

He decided to confide in President Dourad. A few years ago, they had defended each other in battle and worked side by side to establish the central government after Maimun's fall. Most of all, he believed his country's president to be a man of honor.

Sharif explained about the events at the mall. At the same time, he eased the truck past the highway patrolman.

''I have heard nothing about this pair,'' Abdul said when he finished. ''However, we both know that a man who is dispossessed, like Zahad, may be tempted to seek power on his own.''

''I am concerned above all for my son's welfare,'' Sharif said. ''Therefore I have agreed to meet with my cousins.''

As he moved ahead, the patrol car signaled a lane change. Before it could move into the clear space behind the truck, however, a convertible carrying two men in baseball caps zipped up on Sharif's tail.

''Be careful, my friend,'' said the president. ''We need your wisdom and your loyalty in Alqedar. Here, we sit always on a powder keg.''

It was an apt analogy, considering yesterday's blast at the motel. "I have no intention of becoming a casualty," he reassured the president.

They exchanged the traditional wish for peace, and Sharif clicked off. Behind him, the convertible switched to a faster lane and started to pass him. As it went by, the passenger glanced at the sheikh, did a double take and began waving excitedly at the CHP officer.

He had just been recognized.

GROGGILY, Holly opened her eyes. For a disoriented moment, she stared around her. What were they doing parked among tall buildings? Unless she was mistaken, they'd reached downtown Santa Ana, the county seat.

"You awake?" Trevor lifted a strand of hair from her forehead. "Wow, it's hard to get used to you as a brunette, but I guess the red will grow back."

"Where are we?"

"While we were driving, I got an idea." He reached into the back seat for his briefcase. "Guess what I've been carrying around with me all this time?"

She had no idea.

"Remember our marriage license?" He drew out the paper. "Honey, before we go to the police, I want to make you my wife. I want to be your next of kin so I can take care of you."

Numbly, Holly remembered the sheikh saying that she would be safer under Trevor's protection. But she didn't want to marry him. She didn't love him.

Tucking the documents into his jacket, Trevor

came around and opened her door. "Can you walk? You look kind of shaky."

Holly could only focus on one idea at a time. Right now, it was the problem of walking. "I'm not sure."

"Lean on me." Slipping his arm around her, Trevor helped her up. He'd parked the Cadillac in a pay lot next to a brick building. People scurried along an adjacent sidewalk, heading to and from the county buildings.

Diffuse late-afternoon sunshine warmed the top of Holly's head, and, nearby, a couple of palm trees spread their fronds as if soaking up the rays. Everything looked so normal, but it wasn't.

As Trevor took her arm, she strained to object, and couldn't. Maybe it was the medication that kept diverting her mind, making her focus on what he was saying instead of what she was thinking. In fact, she could barely remember what she wanted to protest about.

"I guess I'm being selfish," he said as they walked. "The last few days have been hell. I don't want to burden you with what I've been through, but I never want to experience anything like that again."

"I'm sorry." Holly knew it was her fault. She could have gone home sooner.

"We have a little time before the clerk's office closes." Trevor escorted her up the steps of the brick building. "I mean, why wait? Who knows when we'll be able to get the church again? Not to mention that you lost your wedding dress. We can invite our friends to a big reception when you're feeling better."

"You want to get married now?" she asked dully.

"Nothing that's happened these past few days has changed how I feel." Trevor's blue eyes were wide as he gazed at her. "Sweetheart, you're going to need me more than ever, and I want to be there for you. I've always taken care of you, haven't I?"

Yes, he had. She did need him. And she owed him more than she could ever repay.

Before she could remember why she still wanted to say no, he led her inside.

# Chapter Fourteen

Both occupants of the convertible were signaling to the CHP officer and pointing at Sharif. He fought down the impulse to stomp on the gas pedal. Fleeing would only make the situation worse.

In his side-view mirror, he saw the patrolman scan the truck for any obvious problems that might have excited the two observers. On the steering wheel, his hands grew slippery. Sooner or later, the officer would get a look at him and make the connection to the most wanted man in Southern California.

If the authorities captured him, at least they might rescue his son, he told himself. He steeled himself against the moment when he would be pulled over.

The driver of the convertible lacked his steadiness. Apparently enraged by the slow response from the CHP officer, the man veered into Sharif's lane so sharply that he almost clipped the truck's front bumper.

*Now he's going to stop dead, right in the middle of heavy freeway traffic. People could get killed.*

As if someone had spoken aloud, the sheikh could see the scenario unfolding. Acting on sheer intuition, he jerked the wheel to the right.

Not an instant too soon. As he pulled into the next lane, the convertible's brake lights flashed and the car fishtailed amid the squeal of tires. Apparently the driver believed he could capture the sheikh simply by cutting him off.

Instead, the truck zipped by in the right lane. The patrolman, on the other hand, hit his own brakes a heartbeat too late and smashed into the convertible.

Metal screamed. Horns blared. Other cars swerved wildly, and someone collided with the back of the CHP cruiser.

Even if he'd wished to stop, Sharif had to keep going or risk causing further accidents. He was glad to note, when he checked the mirror, that the two men in the convertible appeared no worse for wear.

Although the patrolman had probably radioed in his license number, for the moment Sharif was free. Even if an all-points bulletin were issued, it hardly mattered, since he didn't intend to keep the truck for long.

Should Zahad prove to be loyal, they would leave the country tonight. Otherwise, he conceded reluctantly, his best course would be to turn himself in.

If, of course, he survived the next few hours.

"HE WILL KILL US," Amy said. "You are crazy to go through with this. We should return to Alqedar at once."

"I must see him." Zahad knew from his own bitterness toward his father that, in some cases, time worked not as a healer but as a slow poison. "I will not leave a job half done."

They had arranged with a young man to trade the motorcycle and a few hundred dollars for a very old car. During a conversation that consisted of as few words as possible, neither side had offered ownership papers.

"It is not a question of an unfinished job." Static electricity made strands of Amy's frosted hair stand away from her head, giving her a frazzled appearance. "We can straighten matters later, when heads are cooler."

"And when his aim is even better?" Zahad couldn't resist asking. He glanced into the back seat, where Amy had placed the baby in a car seat she'd bought. At this angle, he couldn't see Ben, but at least the baby wasn't crying.

They were stopped for a red light in Fullerton when his cell phone rang. "Yes?"

"Do you know how to get to the California State University campus?" Sharif didn't bother to identify himself.

"I believe we are close to it," Zahad said. "We are on Chapman Avenue, just off the freeway."

"Go north on State College Boulevard," said the gruff voice of the man who had been his closest friend all his life. "Turn right on Dorothy Lane, then left and park in front of the gymnasium. Call me when you get there and I will give you further instructions."

"I understand."

"Well?" asked Amy when he folded the phone away.

"It is going to be a traveling show," said Zahad, and set out to follow his cousin's directions.

SHARIF LEFT the truck in a visitor parking area a block past the gym. In the late afternoon, this part of the campus looked deserted, although he could hear the *pock-pock* of tennis balls from outlying courts.

The sports center fronted on a plaza, which separated it from the parking strip to which he'd directed his cousins. For himself, Sharif chose a position out of sight around the side of the gym.

He'd driven around the campus twice, watching for anyone who might be following him and guardedly reassured that no one was. Zahad and Amy together presented danger enough without the wild-card gunman.

Then he'd searched for an isolated spot within the modern campus, with its green stretches of lawn and tall buildings. In case gunfire broke out, he preferred to have as few bystanders as possible.

He stationed himself in an alcove and took out his cell phone. Pretending to use the instrument provided an excuse for standing here, should anyone notice.

As he studied his surroundings and waited for Zahad to call, a breeze brought the fresh scent of flowers. The perfume reminded him of Holly.

The last time he'd seen her, outside the lawyer's office, fiery lights had glimmered in her amber eyes. She'd been so angry at him and so brave, to declare her love in the face of his rejection.

The longing to call her back, to admit he was feigning indifference, had been strong. Even now, Sharif wasn't certain how he'd managed to resist.

He would never forget the joy he'd experienced when he held her. Without realizing it, the grief he'd felt over Yona's death had faded, to be replaced by something new and wonderful.

As a white delivery van jounced over a speed bump alongside the gym, Sharif admitted to himself that after nine years, his sorrow for his late wife had been kept alive by guilt. He was haunted by the sense that he'd failed her because he hadn't been there when she cried out for him in her last, desperate moments.

A buzz in his ear startled him. He pressed the Start button on the phone. "You are in front of the gym?"

"Affirmative," said Zahad.

"Amy and Ben are with you?"

"Yes."

The sheikh's heart rate speeded. His actions during the next few minutes might spell the difference between safety and death for his child.

"Bring them with you," he said. "You are going for a little walk."

AMY INSISTED on changing the baby's diaper, which had become soiled. The delay was driving Zahad crazy.

"Sharif will think we are pulling a trick!" he snapped as she bent over the child in the back seat.

Amy had been right about one thing, he reflected grimly. Sharif wouldn't hesitate to kill them if he thought it would protect his son.

Right now, they were in the worst possible position. His cousin knew exactly where they were, and they had no idea where he was.

Their orders were to proceed to their left and around the side of the building. The route would take them through an open plaza that offered no cover. Where was the sheikh waiting? Was this an ambush?

"Do you see a trash can around here?" Amy asked.

"Forget trash cans! Throw it on the ground!" he said.

"We are in California. If you pollute their environment, helicopters materialize from midair and bomb you," she responded.

Seeing that she wouldn't budge, he checked around furiously. "There is one straight ahead. We will walk right by it."

"Excellent."

She lifted the baby into the cloth carrier, moving unhurriedly. Zahad had never met anyone so infuriating. He remembered now why they had never gotten along.

Nevertheless, they had to work together if they intended to survive. Setting aside his irritation, he scanned the area. He saw no likely hiding places in an athletic field across the way, but Sharif might have taken up a position on the roof of the gym or inside one of the other parked vehicles.

"We have to cross this open space," he said, and added sarcastically, "I hope you remembered to wear body armor."

"As a matter of fact, I did," she said.

"You are joking, right?" He regarded her placid face with disbelief.

"Not at all. I put it on in the airport rest room." She adjusted the pouch. "It's heavy, and it's hot. You are lucky it is not the wrong time of the month for me, or you would be bleeding in several places."

"Did you bring a weapon, also?" He meant the question to be ironic.

Again, she responded coolly. "Yes, and it was not easy smuggling it in my suitcase. Do not ask for details."

It occurred to Zahad as they set out across the plaza that he should have kept a closer eye on Amy back in Alqedar. He was beginning to suspect that he and Sharif might both have underestimated her.

THEY WERE taking too long. Sharif debated dodging from his alcove to another location in case one of his cousins was circling the building. But there was no other cover at hand.

He concentrated on listening for the scuff of shoes or the gurgle of a baby. Even in such a quiet area, it was not easy. The silence was broken by the distant hum of traffic, the rumble of an unidentified motor farther down the drive, and voices exchanging friendly insults on the tennis courts.

The sheikh had chosen not to maintain an open phone line because, while one cousin kept him talking, the other might locate him by the sound of his voice. Now he wished he had kept the line open and demanded that they both talk. He wished a lot of things, including that he had never trusted them in the first place.

Then he heard the footsteps, coming his way. Next to the man's soft rubber soles, the woman's high heels tapped impatiently on the sidewalk. He also heard, or thought he heard, the soft breathing of a baby, but he might have been imagining it.

Sharif steadied his gun.

"Is this where we are to wait?" he heard Amy say in Baharalik, perhaps twenty feet from the alcove.

"He did not specify. I think he wants us to keep walking."

"You should have asked him! In these shoes, I did not expect to be going for a hike!" She sounded so much like the girl he'd grown up with that Sharif nearly stepped out to greet her.

He loved his two quarrelsome cousins. He would have laid down his life for them. Silently, he asked fate to let them be innocent.

"I can hear nothing with your tongue wagging!" Zahad growled, still out of sight. "He might be targeting us right now!"

"Don't be silly. He can't shoot around corners," said Amy, and stepped in the view, facing Sharif. "Here he is. Didn't you see the toe of his shoe sticking out? You men are so puffed up with your own cleverness that you ignore the obvious!"

The reality of seeing his female cousin standing there, her chin uptilted and one arm around Ben in the cloth carrier, made the scene at the mall seem like a hallucination. Realizing that he couldn't shoot her anyway without endangering his son, Sharif lowered his weapon.

Zahad appeared, uncertainty flickering in his eyes. For a long moment, the three of them stood speechless.

It was Amy who spoke first. "Do you want your son now, or shall I carry him for you?"

The sheikh found his voice. "Is he all right?" He didn't dare spend more than a fraction of a second regarding his son, not when he was so vulnerable to attack.

"Oh, he is doing very well since Amy changed his diaper," Zahad said. "It was a major production, complete with an orchestra and dancers. That is what took us so long."

His cousin's grouchy exaggeration made Sharif smile. If these two were traitors, they were also the best actors he'd ever met.

Maybe he was a fool, but he trusted them. Sharif released a long breath and tucked his gun away.

Then, on the periphery of his awareness, he noted something amiss. A sound that wasn't quite right.

Instinctively, he yanked Amy and the baby into the alcove, just as he identified the whump! of a delivery van hitting a speed bump too fast.

The vehicle whined toward them from the recesses of the campus. Bullets snicked off the building.

Frantically, Sharif reached for his gun. Had his cousins set him up? Had he maneuvered himself into their trap?

"Stay back!" Zahad, his weapon drawn, thrust himself in front. At that instant, a bullet meant for the sheikh caught his aide in the shoulder and hurled him to the ground.

Crouching, Sharif returned fire. Past the gym, the delivery van swung in a U-turn and headed back.

"You idiot! Come back here!" Amy, who had set the baby down, crawled partway out onto the pavement, gun in hand.

"No. I will not let him get away." Sharif dodged forward to the cover of a small tree. Through the open side door of the van, he could see the lone occupant struggling to keep the vehicle on course while he reloaded his automatic.

"Fine! I'll stop him!" said his female cousin, and blasted the tires into flapping strips of rubber.

As the van lurched toward a vacant playing field, its driver bailed out. Firing a wild volley in their direction, he landed with a thud.

Sharif leveled his gun and squeezed the trigger. In the stream of bullets, the assailant jerked and dropped his weapon.

For a frozen moment, the sheikh studied the man who would have killed him. He had never met Yusuf Gozen, but he recognized the man from newsclips.

Yusuf was no more than thirty, which meant he had spent most of his adult life seeking to avenge his evil brother. Hatred had eaten away at him as surely as a cancer, leaving an emaciated frame. Only the loathing in his eyes still blazed with vigor.

The man collapsed. But he wasn't dead yet.

Ignoring Zahad's hoarse shout of warning, the sheikh leaped forward. His foot met the dropped gun an instant before Yusuf's hand could close over it, and lobbed it into the field.

With a voice that grew weaker by the second, the man cursed him. He knew he was dying, but he would make no peace in this life.

"Why?" Sharif demanded. "Why did you kill Jasmine, and Noreen Wheaton, and Manuel Estrellas? Why did you grab Holly?"

The assassin spat onto the pavement. "I do not know these people."

He didn't believe him. "You were trying to kill my son."

"A baby? It is nothing." The man's body shook with a cough. Sharif might have felt pity, were he not so aware of the trail of blood this man had left. Even now, Zahad lay injured.

He needed facts to clear his own name, and he had little time before death or the police intervened, so he tried a different tack. "How did you find me?"

"A little luck and a little technology." The man's thin face twisted. "Tell Mrs. Haroun to look in her bag." He tried to suck in a breath but stopped in midgasp.

"Yusuf?" Sharif touched the man, then felt for a pulse. There was none.

He said a brief prayer. It saddened him that a human being had gone to his Maker with only ugliness in his soul.

On the walkway, Zahad sat propped against the wall. Amy held a makeshift compress to his shoulder. "Is he dead?" she asked as the sheikh approached.

"Yes. How is your patient?"

"I'm fine." Zahad brushed the matter aside. "Who is that man?"

"Yusuf Gozen, Maimun's brother." Sharif was glad to see color in his cousin's face, and not too much blood on the compress.

"I heard what he said." With one hand, Amy held out a small metallic disc. "This was in my bag. A tracking device. He must have planted it there at the airport."

"There was a spy," Sharif said. "A man who worked as an airline steward. He was captured yesterday."

Zahad cocked an eyebrow questioningly.

"President Dourad is on our side," Sharif said. "He informed me personally."

"That is wonderful." Irony laced Amy's tone. "I'm sure you would love to stay and chat about your friends in high places, but now, you must go. I have called the paramedics, and no doubt the police will be curious as to the source of the gunshots."

"What is the point of running?" he said. "Now that he is dead..."

"If Yusuf didn't kill those people, someone else did, for a reason we still do not understand." She regarded him steadily. "Who is to say that other killer is not targeting Holly?"

"She's in good hands," he said. "Her fiancé has military experience, and he is taking her to the police."

"Are you so certain they can protect her against someone who has killed three times?"

Her words chilled him. "No." The sheikh's gaze went to the alcove, where his son lay waving his arms and legs lustily. "But my first duty..."

"Is to your people, as is ours," Amy said. "Well, they can wait a little longer. Will you trust me with the boy?"

His cousins had risked their lives to defend Sharif. There was no longer any question of their loyalty. "Of course," he said. "There is, however, one other problem."

"And that is?"

"My truck has been identified."

She reached into Zahad's pocket and, ignoring his sputter of indignation, pulled out a set of keys. "It is a blue American-made sedan, old and battered," she said. "We parked where you told us to."

"Do you really mean to run after that woman?" Zahad demanded. "This is not your fight. Let her own people take care of her."

"You must understand," the sheikh said. "I left Yona to die, alone and in anguish. I will not do this to Holly."

"My brother." Zahad regarded him with unaccustomed gentleness. "Have you tortured yourself over this? Selima and I were both with your wife." After a couple of painful coughs, he forged ahead. "She fell asleep, and slipped from unconsciousness into death.''

''It's true,'' Amy said. ''I saw her face afterward. She was at peace. Sharif, I told you this long ago.''

''I did not believe you.''

A siren wailed along State College Boulevard, a block away. ''Thanks. To you both.'' Without waiting for a response, Sharif hurried toward the back of the building. To avoid the police, he would cut through the campus and approach the car from the far side.

As he strode along, he realized that a darkness had been dispelled deep within him. Someone was sitting with Yona, holding her hand. She was smiling as she fell asleep.

Nothing would change his regret that he had not been there to comfort her. But at least he knew she had not died in despair.

Now he must figure out how to reach Holly. And how to save her from an enemy whose name he still did not know.

# *Chapter Fifteen*

It wasn't until Sharif landed on the freeway in rush-hour traffic that he had time to think about anything beyond eluding the police. Then, stuck in a galaxy of red brake lights, he stared into the rapidly falling darkness and tried to figure out who might want to harm Holly, and why.

There'd been clues pointing in too many directions because of Yusuf. Now it was time to reexamine the facts from a fresh perspective, eliminating the sniper attacks that had been perpetrated by Yusuf.

He must also search for a motive. If it wasn't revenge for Maimun's death, what was it?

Fact: Shortly after sending her son to Holly, Jasmine had gone to meet someone she believed would pay her a lot of money. Instead, she'd been murdered.

Fact: Right after Jasmine's body was discovered, someone had abducted the clinic director and killed her, too.

Possible connection: Had coconspirators in some sort of scheme panicked and turned against each other?

Fact: During Manuel's meeting with Holly, the killer had planted a bomb in his van. Then a masked man had tried to abduct Holly.

Possible connection: Eliminating witnesses who might have damning information about the surrogacy clinic?

That suggested Dr. Lowrie. If he'd been embezzling money and cooking the books, it would give him a reason to eliminate Noreen and Manuel. Perhaps Jasmine, too, if he believed she'd stumbled upon the truth.

But the doctor was in his sixties and somewhat overweight, nothing like the muscular masked man at the motel. Of course, it was possible Lowrie had hired someone to do his dirty work.

As the traffic began to move, Sharif forced himself to pick holes in his theory. It seemed unlikely that the doctor could have hired the same man to kill three people on separate occasions and under different circumstances. And surely, if Manuel had known about an embezzlement, he would have told the police.

Perhaps someone had killed Jasmine for a different reason and then eliminated the others as possible witnesses. But once the first murder was discovered, wouldn't it have been wiser to lie low than to run around planting a bomb and trying to snatch Holly in plain daylight?

Simply covering up past wrongdoing didn't seem like enough of a motive. But what else could it be?

In any case, Sharif needed to warn Holly that she, and not he himself, might now be the killer's prime target. She needed round-the-clock police protection.

The traffic thinned south of Fullerton, then clogged again at an interchange with two other freeways. He was getting nowhere fast.

With a spurt of alarm, the sheikh realized he didn't

even know where Holly was. He'd been driving toward the coast by instinct, not by plan.

Most likely, he reminded himself, Trevor had taken Holly directly to the police. But as a kidnap victim in the public's eye, she wasn't likely to be arrested immediately even if charges were pending. And if she were, her fiancé would promptly arrange bail.

Was she at Trevor's house? Would even a state-of-the-art alarm system be enough to keep out a determined predator?

Adrenaline pumped inside him. He had to find Holly.

All these years, Sharif had held in check his need for a wife and a family. But Holly had bypassed his defenses with her courage and her intelligence and her instinctive sensuality. He loved her, and regardless of whether she married him or Trevor, he needed above all to protect her.

How could he reach her? She had no cell phone, and Trevor's home number would be unlisted. He did remember Hoolihan's office number, though. The lawyer could relay a warning.

When his lane idled again, Sharif dialed. After three rings, an answering machine picked up. "The law office of Edward Hoolihan has closed for the day. If this is an emergency, please page him at..."

He input the pager number and entered that of his cell phone. During the next few minutes, using the phone whenever the traffic stopped, Sharif got Trevor Samuelson's office number from information, dialed his recording and paged him as well.

No one was calling back, however. Who else might know how to find her?

Alice Frey, the sheikh thought. A close friend as

well as employer, she would be in touch with Holly if anyone were.

Unlike a law office, a beauty salon didn't close at five o'clock. She might still be there.

Now that he'd cleared the interchange, traffic was moving too fast for him to dial information. Besides, how likely was Alice to give him the information over the phone?

Risky as it was, he preferred to contact her in person.

A SENSE OF unreality clung to Holly as Trevor opened the front door of his sprawling, one-story home. "I'd carry you over the threshhold, honey, but first I'd better disable the alarm," he said.

"I... It's okay." She bit back her explanation that the sedative was having an unsettling effect on her stomach. It would be rude to keep complaining, as if she didn't appreciate all he'd done for her.

She missed Sharif more with every passing minute. In her dazed state, she kept imagining he would appear and take her away, to the cabin or a tent—anywhere but here.

The hall light shimmered off the diamond ring on her finger. It was gorgeous, and last week she'd been impressed beyond words when Trevor took her to a jeweler to select it. Now she wished it would disappear.

Had they really said their vows this afternoon and signed their names at the county clerk's office? It didn't feel like a wedding, not with her wearing jeans and having trouble keeping her eyes open. Not when her heart belonged to a man she might never see again.

Trevor kept acting as if he expected Holly to be the

same person as before. Well, of course he did. How could he know how much her feelings had changed?

She didn't want to be married to him. She wasn't sure why she'd spoken the words, why she hadn't objected during the brief ceremony.

She'd been struggling to stand upright, and somehow whenever Trevor prompted her to say something, she'd repeated his words automatically. The medication must have taken control of whichever part of the brain controlled the tongue.

Inside the marble-floored entryway, she tried to get her bearings. To the left, she remembered, were Trevor's home office, the kitchen and laundry facilities, and the unoccupied maid's quarters.

Straight ahead lay the living room and, past it, a cliffside terrace that she'd admired on her previous visits. Sheltered by the house and a high stone wall with a locked wrought-iron gate, it revealed a vista of shoreline and shining ocean. But right now, Holly had no interest in anything except finding a bathroom.

She stumbled to her right, toward the bedroom wing. "Are you okay?" Trevor called as he input his code into the alarm box. "You don't look too steady."

"I just want to lie down." She glanced back apologetically.

He remained standing in the faint glow of security lights. "Maybe if I fix you something to eat, you'll feel better."

Further conversation was beyond her. "Sure," Holly mumbled, and stumbled toward the nearest bathroom.

When she got there, she emptied the contents of

her stomach. That made her feel a little better, and washing up helped, too.

What she really needed was a nap and a shower, although, even after she reached the master bedroom, she couldn't figure out in which order. Before she could decide, the intercom buzzed.

What was she supposed to do? Oh, right, press the button over the end table. Would she ever get used to living in this house?

But Holly didn't intend to live here. Even though Sharif was gone, she didn't see how she could ever sleep with another man.

Sharif. Gone. Was he safe? Would she ever know?

She wished she'd stayed with him, no matter how dangerous it was. But he'd said he didn't want her. It might even be true.

Stumbling to the wall, she pushed the button. "Yes?"

It was Trevor, speaking from the kitchen. "Listen, hon, after we eat, let's take a dip in the Jacuzzi and enjoy the stars. We both need to unwind."

The terrace's centerpiece was a whirlpool bath. The hot spa water combined with the bracing air might help to revive her. "Okay."

"Go ahead and put on your swimsuit."

"Aren't we eating first?" she asked.

"There's no law against having dinner in your swimsuit."

"I—guess not." The intercom clicked off.

Although he'd seen her in a bikini before, Holly found herself reluctant to reveal that much of herself to Trevor tonight.

He was her husband. But not in her heart.

Forcing herself to keep moving despite her weariness, she opened the bureau drawer where she'd put some of her clothes. Thank goodness there was an old one-piece suit along with the bikini.

She wiggled into it, and stuck her feet into a pair of flip-flops. From the hall linen closet, she retrieved a beach towel.

In the corridor, she couldn't resist glancing into the bedroom they'd fixed up for Ben. The sight of the empty crib sent her heart slamming into her ribs. Where was her baby? What had those people done to him?

Holly leaned against the doorframe, on the verge of tears. For hours now, she'd been trying not to think about Ben, when she'd been coherent enough to think at all. Trying not to worry, knowing she could do nothing.

Fear and longing washed over her like a tidal wave. She couldn't go to dinner and pretend she was a happy bride.

"Honey?" Trevor appeared at her side, although she hadn't heard his footsteps. No wonder; he was, she saw, barefoot. He must have changed into his swimsuit in one of the bathrooms, and now she got an unobstructed view of his well-built chest and its mat of blond hair. "Wow, you're out of it, aren't you? Come on, I'll help you."

There was no point in protesting. Besides, she found that she couldn't. Once again, she could only focus on his voice and what he was telling her to do.

She might as well lean on him. She'd been doing it for years, hadn't she?

THE ONLY shop still alight in the small center was the Sunshine Lane Salon. Sharif cruised past, watching for undercover police.

He saw no one. Perhaps Harbor View's homicide detectives had already been called to Fullerton to interview Amy and Zahad.

Pulling into the lot, the sheikh parked just outside the circle of light that spilled from the building. If anyone asked him, he planned to say he was waiting for his girlfriend.

Except for fewer than half a dozen cars clustered by the salon, the place was deserted. Sitting here in the dark, awaiting a chance to speak to Mrs. Frey, gave Sharif time to reflect.

This was where Holly and Jasmine had worked. He could picture them joking as they crossed the blacktop together, heading for a day of cutting and perming and whatever else women did to their hair.

If only he'd never entered their lives, both of them would be safe. At least, he assumed they would. Even though he now knew that Jasmine's killer was not Yusuf, it was to bear Sharif's baby that she'd been recruited at the surrogacy center. And it was the clinic that linked her to the other deaths.

As he watched a tall well-coiffed woman emerge and unlock her car, he wondered if it were possible he'd gotten the scenario backward. What if Jasmine had been recruited by someone who already had an ulterior motive? What if the situation hadn't started with the clinic...

Before he could pursue this line of speculation, another lady departed. Lights flicked off inside, and then two women in casual clothing emerged. Judging by their rumpled appearance, they were employees rather than patrons.

There was only one person still visible through the glass front, a short middle-aged woman. Alice, he thought, although he'd only glimpsed her on Monday. She fussed around, turning off appliances and the remaining lights.

One of the employees pulled out of the lot. The other, whose tangle of blond hair looked as if she'd slept on it, lingered inside her vehicle, fooling with the radio or the glove box.

If she didn't leave before Alice came out, he would have to risk contacting her in front of a witness. That was a complication Sharif would prefer to avoid.

The owner emerged and locked the door. After waving to the blonde, she strolled toward her Mercedes.

The employee finished fiddling around and backed out slowly. She stopped, then backed some more. It seemed like eons before she straightened and drove onto the street.

Alice beeped the remote for her car. Lights and door locks sprang to life, ready to provide swift admittance to the owner.

Not wanting to panic her by jumping out, Sharif rolled down his window. "Alice!"

She turned. "Who is it?"

"Holly needs your help!" he called. "She's in danger!"

"Zahad? Is that you?"

The name startled him, until he remembered that his cousin had contacted her. "No, it's Sharif. Zahad's been shot, but he'll be all right."

She stood clutching her oversize handbag as if her life depended on it. He wondered if she carried some kind of defensive spray. "I thought Holly was with you," she challenged.

"She's with her fiancé," he said. "She went back to him this afternoon."

"And the baby? Does she have him?"

The intensity in the woman's voice startled him. He hadn't realized she was so strongly attached to Ben. "No. He's with Zahad and my cousin Amy. I presume the police are questioning them."

"Will they be arrested? You can't let that little boy be taken to the children's home!" Alice didn't seem to have registered his concern for Holly. "He'd be so frightened!"

"They have no reason to do that. He's in Amy's care, and she's not under suspicion." That wasn't quite true, since she'd been packing a gun, but he couldn't afford to waste time. "We have to get a warning to Holly."

The woman blinked. "Oh, yes, you mentioned that. But you said she's with Trevor, didn't you?"

"They were supposed to meet at a lawyer's office. Have you heard from her today?"

She shook her head.

"Well, we need to tell them that the killer isn't who we thought it was. And for all we know, he may be after her." Sharif hoped this abbreviated explanation would suffice for now. "Do you have Trevor Samuelson's address or phone number?"

"It might be in my purse." Alice moved toward the car. A motherly woman, she reminded him of his aunt Selima.

Opening her handbag, she reached inside. It occurred to Sharif that he shouldn't be leaning out toward her this unguardedly. But what harm could she do?

TREVOR'S KITCHEN had been designed by his former wife, who'd run a part-time catering business specializing in desserts. Karen had included an industrial-strength array of gleaming counters, steel sinks and freestanding islands, and a double set of dishwashers.

In the hands of a bachelor, the place probably didn't see much use. Even tonight, Trevor's idea of a fancy meal was to set out several trays of deli food, along with a bottle of champagne.

When Holly entered, he handed her a filled glass. "I want to propose a toast."

"A toast?"

"Hey, honey, try to act like you just got married, okay?"

Embarrassed, she accepted the glass. "I'm sorry."

"Let's do this properly." Leaning close, he entwined their wrists.

The touch of Trevor's forearm against hers made Holly uncomfortably aware of his bare chest and legs, inches away. He was a good-looking man and an old friend. But he wasn't Sharif.

"To us," he said. "To the future." His blue eyes regarded her steadily. "Go on, take a sip. It's for luck."

Although Holly felt none too steady, she didn't want to disappoint him. She swallowed a mouthful, letting the bubbles pop against the back of her throat. It settled her stomach a bit, so she took another sip.

"Good girl." To her relief, Trevor finished his glass and moved away. "Hey, here's something special I saved." From a second refrigerator, he retrieved their tiered wedding cake. "It might be a little stale, but it should taste good."

"How—romantic." She gave him a quavery smile.

He'd gone to so much trouble that she didn't want to risk getting sick in the middle of the kitchen. "Could you excuse me a minute?"

"The powder room's through my office." He regarded her with concern. "Maybe I shouldn't have given you that sedative. I thought it would wear off by now."

"It—is wearing off." She set down her glass and hurried through his office to the bathroom.

Her stomach wasn't as upset as she'd thought, and she found she didn't need to use the facilities. After a few minutes, she ventured out.

From the kitchen, she could hear Trevor whistling. Good. He deserved a break from the week's tension.

In his office, she inhaled the fragrance of pine wall paneling. This room, more than any other in the house, reflected Trevor's interests and accomplishments, from the shelf of golf trophies to the framed photos showing him with county and state political figures.

Straightening her shoulders, Holly prepared to go back into the kitchen. Something caught her eye, and she paused.

A couple of silver dollars had been tossed into a souvenir plate from Las Vegas. Trevor must have picked them up during a convention. But was it the coins that had commanded her attention, or the red Overdue stamp on the envelope tucked behind it?

The return address was that of a utility company. Trevor might delay paying a bill if it were in dispute, but why would he be late with a routine household payment?

Maybe he simply wasn't as well organized at home as at his office. Anyway, she was in no condition to worry about finances right now.

Goose bumps formed on Holly's skin when she emerged into the kitchen. Thanks to the tile, the air felt five degrees colder than in the office, and she was wearing very little.

"Hey, you look half-frozen." Trevor stood behind the counter, arms spread, hands resting on the edge. "How's your stomach?"

With shaky fingers, she tucked some hair behind her ear. "Better."

"Thank goodness that pill's finally wearing off," he said. "I'm going to give Alice a piece of my mind next time I see her. That's not what I call a mild sedative."

The room tilted, and Holly grabbed the back of a chair to keep her balance. "M-maybe I spoke too soon. Or are we having an earthquake?"

"Not that I've noticed. You okay?"

"Sh-shouldn't have drunk the champagne, I guess." Although she'd only taken a few sips, the alcohol must be interacting with the remains of the sedative. "I need to—lie down."

"Let's relax in the Jacuzzi." He came and slipped his arm around her waist. It felt strong, intimate, and controlling.

Holly barely had time to snatch her towel from the counter before Trevor guided her through the breakfast room, out the French doors and onto the terrace. When her knees threatened to give way, she leaned against him.

Cold air blasted against her exposed skin. Shivering, she hurried beside her husband toward the illuminated circle of steaming spa water.

## Chapter Sixteen

From her purse, Alice lifted a small black rectangle. For a startled moment, Sharif thought she was going to shoot him or spray him, and then he realized it was a leather-bound book.

"Darn," she said as she flipped through it. "I thought I entered her new address, but it's not here. I've been to Trevor's house and I could probably find it if we drove around, but I can't tell you exactly where it is."

"How about a phone number?"

She squinted at a page. "It's not here, either. Now, let me see. I talked to him Tuesday night, so I must have it. No, that's wrong. He's the one who called me."

The night lay chilly and silent around them. To Sharif, it seemed filled with menace. Someone might be closing in on Holly, even as they stood here talking.

"I must reach her," he said. "Perhaps my caution is excessive, but I don't believe so."

"Why do you think this killer would come after her?" Alice asked.

"Right after the bombing that killed Manuel Estrellas, a masked man tried to kidnap her,'' he said. ''There must be something she knows or that he believes she knows. Something this man wants to hide.''

Alice dropped the address book back into her bag. ''I feel horrible about what happened to Manuel.''

''You didn't actually know him, did you?''

''No, but I'm the one who told you where to find him. That makes me partly responsible.''

Sharif struggled to grasp a dangling thread, a connection that might involve Alice and the bombing and Holly. ''Did you give anyone else information about him? The killer must have followed Manuel to the motel, but we don't know how he picked up the trail in the first place.''

Even in the diffuse glow of a streetlamp, he could see the change in Alice's expression. Her jaw went slack, and she blinked rapidly. ''Only…Trevor.''

The implication hit hard. Still, he didn't want to jump to conclusions. ''Why did Trevor say he wanted Manuel's phone number?''

She spoke thickly. ''Not just his phone number. His address, too. Something about covering his bases in case Manuel turned out to be dangerous.''

Samuelson was tough and in good physical shape, like the masked man at the motel. Nevertheless, the attacker had done more than just grab Holly. ''I doubt a lawyer would know how to wire a car bomb. Doing it quickly, without drawing attention—that would take an expert.''

Alice had a hard time swallowing before she replied, ''Special forces. He was in some kind of special forces with Holly's father in the army.''

Special forces. Demolition? At the very least, the

man would have a nodding acquaintance with terrorists and their methods.

Murder wouldn't be difficult for a man with his background, not if he had the right motive. Whatever that might be.

He'd certainly had the opportunity. Jazz would have trusted Trevor, just as Holly did. But what would be his motive? And Noreen Wheaton's connection remained a mystery, one that Sharif knew he couldn't solve right now.

The only thing that mattered was that he'd entrusted Holly to the one person from whom she most needed protecting. He had to find her.

"Let's go." He shoved open the passenger door.

"Me?" Alice squeaked.

"You said you'd know his house if you saw it."

"The police..."

"Will waste precious time nailing me to the wall before they interrupt a respected lawyer at home," he said.

Her hands fluttered in the air, and for a moment he thought she would flee. Then she nodded and got in beside him.

BELOW THE guardrail spread twinkling lights, all the way to the black sweep of the Pacific Ocean. Above, when Holly tilted her head, lay smoky, impenetrable clouds. It was as if the stars had fallen to earth and left the sky empty.

Looking upward had been a mistake, she realized as she clung to Trevor. It made her dizzier.

"Want me to lift you into the pool?" he asked.

"I—guess so."

He caught her by the waist and lowered her onto a

low shelf inside the spa. There was something familiar about his grip. He'd held her this way before, Holly thought, but she couldn't remember when.

*When he threw me over his shoulder.* No, that hadn't been Trevor, it had been the man at the motel.

After nearly wearing off, the effects of the sedative seemed to be getting worse, she found as she sank down on the seat. Was it just the champagne, or could there have been something more in her drink?

But Trevor was her friend, her protector. Even if he were upset for some reason, he wouldn't harm her.

"Trev?" she asked shakily.

"What is it, honey?" The water rippled as he slid in beside her. "Want me to turn on the jets?"

"N-no." She ran her hand over his bare shoulder and the muscular upper arm. When he gazed at her, his eyes glowed blue, like the illuminated water. "Trev, I'm scared."

His smooth confidence yielded to a hint of uncertainty. "Kid, I really do care about you."

"I know." His face went in and out of focus. She blinked, struggling to stay awake.

His hand cupped her chin and moved along her jawline. "Babe, I wish…" The words trailed off, and abruptly his expression hardened. Reaching over, he switched on the jets.

The noise shattered the evening's peace as the currents whipped the water into a frothy brew. "I asked you not to…"

"I like the noise. Don't you?" His tone had a harsh edge. "You know, being a brunette just doesn't suit you. Honey, I don't think this marriage is going to work out."

What was he talking about? Before Holly could get

her bearings, his fingers tangled in the hair at the back of her head and his other hand closed over her arm. She felt herself drawn downward, off-balance, from the ledge into the water.

"Trev!"

"Shut up."

Water closed over her face. Too stunned to protest, she waited for him to release her.

His grip tightened. He was holding her here, underwater. Her lungs started to hurt. What was wrong with him? Why was he doing this?

He wasn't going to let go. Even in her drugged state, she could see that.

He was never going to let her up. Was he trying to kill her?

The pain in her chest tightened into panic. She had to find the surface. Had to take a breath.

Frantically, Holly dug her fingernails into his arm. Adrenaline must have kicked in, because she managed to pinch a small fold of his skin hard enough to break it.

The arm jerked away, and the hold on her hair loosened. In that instant, Holly thrashed to the surface and sucked in a gulp of blessed air.

Suddenly he was back, grabbing her again. She tried to cry out, but began coughing instead.

He cursed at her, his face distorted with anger. Who was this man? What had happened to the Trevor she thought she knew?

Those rugged arms shoved her down. Holly tried to wrench free, but she felt like she was fighting in a vacuum.

Over the din of the spa jets, she heard a hard metallic rattle. Was someone climbing the wrought-iron gate?

Mercifully, Trevor released her. Holly's head broke water and she scrabbled against the slippery tile floor until she landed on a shelf at the far side.

Blurrily, she made out a man in dark clothes, zig-zagging across the terrace. For a disoriented moment, she thought it was the masked kidnapper from the motel. But that must have been Trevor.

Then she recognized the lean power of this man's build. It was Sharif, and he had a gun.

While he paused to take aim, Trevor ducked forward, using Holly as cover. At the same time, his arm skimmed across the water and sent a sheet of water flying through the air.

Instinctively, Sharif dodged. Bolting from the pool, Trevor slammed into him.

They wrestled for the gun, two trained men with no holds barred. Beyond, on the street, a police siren wailed, but it seemed impossibly far away.

Holly tried to scrabble out of the spa, to help Sharif, but she didn't have the strength. She could barely keep her head above water.

One of the men flung the other to the ground, and was hauled down with him. She heard the crunch of heads butting and grunts of pain.

Outside the gate, a male voice shouted, ''Police! Put your hands up!'' Two shots blasted off the lock.

Sharif and Trevor faced each other, panting. Midway between them, on the concrete, lay the gun.

''Hands in the air! Both of you!'' Two officers thrust their way through the gate. They were followed by a woman whom Holly couldn't see clearly.

Slowly, the combatants obeyed. Sharif's gaze went to Holly. "Are you all right?"

She started to nod. Then she heard Trevor's voice, rough, authoritative. "Officers, this man attacked me and my wife. He's the killer you've been looking for."

Both officers kept their weapons drawn. "We'll sort this out at the station, Mr. Samuelson," one of them said.

The respect in his voice alarmed Holly. Despite the policeman's words, she doubted he understood how dangerous Trevor was. "He—" She pointed at the man who was her husband. "He tried to—" Some water came up, and she broke off, coughing.

"My wife needs an ambulance," Trevor snapped. "Cuff this man and call the paramedics."

"Don't believe him!" The woman moved into view. It was Alice. "Trevor Samuelson's your murderer, Officer Williams. I drove here with Sheikh Al-Khalil to save Holly, and by the look of things, we barely got here in time."

The policeman kept his attention fixed on Trevor. "The homicide sergeant called from Fullerton and sent us over here. He found out Ms. Rivers was supposed to have surfaced this afternoon and he wondered why the police weren't notified. I guess he was suspicious of you, too, Mr. Samuelson."

Trevor exhaled impatiently. "This whole thing is a misunderstanding." Then, so quickly no one had time to react, he swooped onto the gun, rolled across the ground and fired at Sharif.

But the sheikh wasn't there. He'd leaped in front of Holly to shield her. Stunned, she heard more shots, hard and fast.

"Sharif?" she cried.

He was still crouched in front of her. After a moment, he turned and reached to help her up. "Don't look," he said.

"Is he—?" she managed to ask through the dimness in her brain.

"You won't have to worry about him anymore," murmured Sharif, and gathered her into his arms, dripping wet.

"Mr. Al-Khalil? Release the woman and put your hands up." The command came from overhead.

"Yes, officer." Cautiously, he let go. Holly sagged onto the concrete, and darkness closed in.

SHE AWOKE in a hospital room. Bouquets crowded the bedside table.

Turning her head on the pillow, Holly saw that the second bed was empty. Beyond it, an arrangement of calla lilies and a potted azalea covered the window ledge. They reminded her of the flowers in the church courtyard. That had been on Monday. And this was…?

She focused on the only other person in the room, a trim man in a business suit. "What day is it?" she asked hoarsely.

"Friday. You slept all night." When he came closer, she recognized the attorney, Edward Hoolihan. "Trevor filled you with sedatives. If he'd given you much more, the drugs alone would have killed you."

"He said…Alice sent them to me."

The lawyer shook his head. "Apparently his former wife left them behind."

As if in a dream, Holly recalled awakening in the night and being attended by a nurse. Other than that, she remembered nothing since she'd collapsed at the spa. "Is Sharif all right?"

"He's fine. So is that cute little nephew of yours. He's quite a charmer." Her visitor smiled for the first time.

"Where are they?"

"The sheikh's still in custody, but I expect he'll be released soon," Hoolihan said. "Zahad Adran is recovering from a gunshot. They have legal counsel from Los Angeles, thanks to the president of Alqedar. Since I'm not representing them anymore, I'd like to offer my services as your attorney, free of charge. You should have counsel when you talk to the police."

"Why are you willing to help me for free?" she repeated in surprise.

"I shouldn't have let Trevor take you out of my office without notifying the police. I'd like to make it up to you," he said. "Do you feel well enough to talk to the detective now? He's waiting in the hall."

Although Holly wasn't sure how coherent she would be, she wanted the authorities to hear her side of the story. "Sure."

In came a plainclothesman who identified himself as homicide Lt. Bill Chavez. With a tape recorder playing and Hoolihan standing by, he led Holly step by step through the events of the past few days.

After describing the attempt to murder her, she said, "Why would Trevor do this? To me and to Jazz?"

At first, she thought Chavez might refuse to answer. Then he said, "With our suspect dead, I can release some information. When we ran a credit check on Mr. Samuelson, which we always do with possible suspects, we found a lot of debts. It turned out he'd been gambling heavily for years.''

"But he never acted like he was broke!"

"He supplemented his income by leasing out the property he was managing for you and your sister," the detective said. "It's chockfull of warehouses."

"He was stealing lease money that should have gone to us?" It was a small betrayal, compared to the other things he'd done, she reflected sadly. "But— did he kill Mrs. Wheaton, too? What was his connection with her?"

"In the clinic's files, we discovered that he'd drawn up some contracts for them," Chavez said. "We also believe he recruited your sister as a surrogate."

"Why?"

"The office manager says Mrs. Wheaton offered a large reward to anyone who located a woman acceptable to the sheikh. We found a canceled check made out to Mr. Samuelson from the clinic for twenty thousand dollars," the policeman said.

Trevor must have lied about the parents and tricked Jazz into having Ben. Holly shivered at the cold-bloodedness of the man she and her sister had both trusted. "If he had financial problems, why didn't he just declare bankruptcy?"

"We hear via some underworld sources that he owed money to people who don't take kindly to being stiffed for debts," the lieutenant said. "There's talk someone was putting out a contract on his life."

The blood drained from Holly's cheeks. She'd been hoping there was some explanation—madness, a brain tumor—that made it possible Trevor had once been the good man she'd believed him to be. Instead, he was the kind of man who'd created a mess and then sacrificed other people's lives to try to save his own.

Alice poked her head in the door. "Can Holly have company?"

"It might be a good idea for her to have a friend at hand," the detective said, waving her inside. "Ms. Rivers, you look pale. Should I call a doctor?"

She swallowed hard. "No. I want to know why Trevor married me. What would he gain by such a marriage?"

Alice sat beside the bed. The touch of her hand on Holly's arm steadied her.

"We talked to the on-site manager at the desert property," the lieutenant said. "According to him, a major developer is interested in buying the land for a discount megamall. He'd have paid millions."

"As my husband, Trevor would control the property with no questions asked," she said slowly.

"Your sister visited the manager a few days before her death, asking a lot of questions," Chavez said. "She must have become suspicious of Mr. Samuelson after she learned he'd lied about the baby's parents."

"She confronted him." Holly knew her sister well enough to figure that Jazz would have taken the most direct course. "So he killed her."

"It's a reasonable supposition," the detective said.

Afterward, Noreen and Manuel must have been murdered in an attempt to cover up the link between Trevor and Jazz, Holly thought.

She remembered the masked man at the motel, and didn't doubt it had been Trevor. In some convoluted way, he must have believed he could win her back by "rescuing" her.

There was one more, terrible question to which she needed an answer. "After he married me, why did he want to kill me?"

From his briefcase, Chavez removed a photocopy of a document labeled Last Will and Testament. "Is this your signature, Ms. Rivers?"

She stared at it in dismay. It was a will leaving all of her possessions to Trevor. The shaky signature at the bottom looked authentic.

"When I was drugged, he gave me something to sign. This must have been..." She couldn't go on. She felt so overwhelmed by grief and pain, she could hardly speak.

"Thank you," said the lieutenant. "I'm sorry this has been so difficult, Ms. Rivers. If we have any further questions, I'll be in touch."

Hoolihan showed him to the door. Exhaustion, and the lingering effects of drugs, forced Holly's eyes shut. She scarcely had time to realize she was falling asleep, before she lost consciousness.

When she awoke, Alice was still there. And one truth had come clear in Holly's mind.

If Sharif hadn't kidnapped her by mistake, Trevor would probably have killed her by now and disguised it as an accident. And if he hadn't raced to her aid yesterday, the police would have arrived a few lethal minutes too late.

She owed him her life and, more than that, she'd given him her heart. Even if he'd acted from a sense of duty, even if he couldn't accept her into his world, she would always love him.

Then Holly noticed a change in the air pressure and a subtle, enticing warmth. Even before she met Sharif's gaze, she knew he'd entered the room.

A white burnoose framed his dark, concerned face, and a creamy robe fell to his ankles. "I am glad to find you awake."

She couldn't help smiling, even though she knew he'd come to say goodbye. "And I'm glad you're out of jail."

"Why the fancy clothes?" Alice asked.

"Amy insisted I wear them to impress the media. They were massed outside the police station." With easy grace, he crossed to Holly's bedside.

"You look impressive," Holly whispered. "Did they ask a lot of questions?"

"Hundreds. I answered the ones that were not too presumptuous." Sitting on the edge of the bed, he took her hands in his. "I have had a busy morning, but soon my son and I must leave for home."

"We'll miss you terribly," she said.

"We?" he murmured.

"*I'll* miss the baby," Alice said tartly. "*She'll* miss you. Well, I might, too, a little. You were a splendid sight yesterday."

"Thank you, Sharif," Holly said. "Without you, I wouldn't be here."

He studied her. "The doctor tells me you can be released if someone will take care of you."

"She's coming home with me," Alice said.

"I fear not." He slid one arm beneath Holly's back, the other under her legs. "She will be traveling with me. If she agrees to be abducted, of course."

"She's in no shape to go anywhere!" her friend chided.

"The president of my country has sent a private jet." The sheikh scooped Holly into the air. "She will have every convenience. And I have heard that love is the best healer.''

She wound her arms around his neck. If this was another dream, she didn't want it to end. ''But you said—''

''I hope you will forgive me for lying about my feelings. I only meant to shield you from harm.'' All trace of joking vanished. ''Holly, I want to marry you. To shower you with beautiful things, and share my life with you, and make you smile a thousand times every day. Please say yes.''

She didn't need to think about it. ''Yes, to all of the above!''

''You still love me?'' he teased.

''Only for as long as the sands blow and the stars shine,'' she said.

''That will do,'' said the sheikh. ''For starters.'' Then he swept her out of the room and into their new life together.

# *Epilogue*

Even through the thick arched window of the palace nursery, Holly could hear the construction noises. Work was proceeding quickly on the hospital.

Sharif's vitality never ceased to amaze her. During the day, he oversaw the production of Jubah cloth and kept tabs on his region's public works. At night, he fulfilled her wildest imaginings.

Female voices drew her attention. She forced herself away from the fascinating sights and sounds of the city below.

"He needs a haircut," Alice was saying. She knelt on a carpet, examining Ben as he played with blocks.

"No, no! Not until he is five!" protested Selima from her low stool.

"His bangs are getting in his eyes." The salon owner frowned at the reddish-brown mop that fell below the toddler's eyebrows.

She was itching to put her stamp on her godson, Holly could see. Ever since Alice arrived for a visit three days earlier, she and Selima had been politely jockeying for favor with the child they both loved.

"We will consult the mother." Folding her hands confidently on her lap, Selima regarded Holly.

She hated to get in the middle of this friendly rivalry. But with Alice and Selima both waiting expectantly, Holly knew she had to take a stand.

"You can cut his bangs," she said. "As a safety measure. But we'll leave the rest till he's five." Letting children's hair grow was a local tradition, one of many that Amy had explained during the six months since Holly and Sharif had married.

The transition to a foreign country had been challenging, and there was a great deal yet to learn. Fortunately, Holly already had two friends in her husband's cousins, and another in Selima. She was even learning to speak Baharalik.

Being surrounded by an extended family helped ease the ache in her heart whenever she thought of her sister. Sharif had been right. Love *was* the best healer.

The two older women nodded in approval. "The wisdom of Solomon," said Selima. "You have pleased us both."

"I can't help noticing how terrific everyone's hair looks in this palace," Alice added. "Unless I miss my guess, Holly's had a hand in that."

"Two hands, and a pair of scissors," agreed Sharif's aunt. "We are very fortunate."

Holly thanked them and, leaving the toddler in their care, went to see if Sharif had returned to the palace for lunch. He tried to join her whenever possible.

In the hallway, she encountered Zahad. Fully recovered from his injury, he nodded to her cheerfully. "You will find your husband in your private quarters," he said. "He asked me to tell you that there is good news."

Glad of a chance to have Sharif to herself, Holly

thanked him and hurried past a tapestried wall. She doubted she would ever take this jewel-like palace for granted.

A side passage led to their private suite. When she stepped inside, she caught a blur of motion from the corner of her eye, and then strong arms pinned her.

"Sharif!"

"Prepare to be conquered," he said, and kissed her thoroughly.

With a happy sigh, Holly hugged him. "What's the good news?"

"The hospital will be completed in less than six months," he said, leaning over her. "Well ahead of schedule."

Holly laughed. "You rushed home to tell me this? It could have waited."

"No, it could not." His lips quirked as he angled her through the sitting room, toward the inner chamber.

"What are you doing?"

"Even allowing for delays, it will open in less than nine months," he said. In his face she read the joy of knowing that no one else would have to die for lack of the best medical facilities.

Caught up in his warmth, Holly took a moment to grasp his meaning. A child! He was finally ready to have a child with her.

Since their marriage, Sharif had insisted on using protection. She'd hoped he would change his mind.

"I'm so glad we can start trying!" Holly said.

He pressed her firmly onto the bed. "A sheikh does not merely try. He pursues his goal single-mindedly until he masters it."

She could hardly wait.